D1391466

BLOOD ON THE RIO GRANDE

BLOOD ON THE RIO GRANDE

Leslie Scott

SAGEBRUSH
Large Print Westerns

Published in Large Print 2009 by ISIS Publishing Ltd.,
7 Centremead, Osney Mead, Oxford OX2 0ES
United Kingdom
by arrangement with
Golden West Literary Agency

British Library Cataloguing in Publication Data
Scott, Leslie, 1893–1975.
    Blood on the Rio Grande [text (large print)].
    1. Western stories.
    2. Large type books.
    I. Title
    813.5'2–dc22

ISBN 978–0–7531–8257–4 (hb)

Printed and bound in Great Britain by
T. J. International Ltd., Padstow, Cornwall

CHAPTER
ONE

From where Lafe Haskins lay at the edge of the pine growth, he could see over the chaparral which clothed the lower slope to the broad grey ribbon of the trail that wound around a jutting cliff a little to the north. From time to time he raised his heavy Winchester to his shoulder and drew the bright bead of the front sight down into the notch until it focused squarely on that shoulder of rock standing out hard and clear in the afternoon sunshine. It was but three hundred yards to the bend in the trail, and the rifle was point-blank at three-fifty.

Haskins was going to kill Jim Grant. When Grant rode around the bend, the rifle would speak, and that would take care of the feud between them for good and all.

Afterward? Haskins wasn't worried. It was a rough country and there were outlaws in the hills who would kill a man for his horse or what his pockets might contain.

Haskins hated Jim Grant, but an even more compelling motive made him determined to get rid of the Swinging J range boss. Grant was in his way. Jim Grant might well bring to naught a certain elaborate

1

scheme Haskins had conceived when he had learned that old Joel Collison had decided to leave the Nueces River country and move to the Rio Grande Valley.

Overhead, the Texas sky was brilliantly blue, with here and there a flecking of white clouds, their edges turning pink as the sun sank lower. Soon the slope would be in the shadow, but the trail would remain bright for a little longer.

Haskins laid his rifle on the ground and waited.

"Looking for somebody, Lafe?"

Haskins' body jerked at the sound of the voice behind him. He screwed his head around and saw Jim Grant standing not three paces distant.

Jim Grant wasn't exactly a small man — just under six feet, and a hundred and eighty pounds — although he looked small beside the hulking Haskins. However, he loomed big to Haskins right then, standing there with his thumbs hooked over his double cartridge belts. He voiced no threat, made no threatening move; he just stood there regarding Haskins, his steady grey eyes narrowed the merest trifle.

But that was enough! Haskins understood perfectly. A single wrong gesture on his part, and those slender hands would dart down and up. Haskins would see the flash of the gun, but he wouldn't hear the report, a slug travelling a bit faster than sound.

Grant finally spoke. "Shove that long gun in front of you," he said. "Now give it a good push."

Haskins obeyed. The rifle slithered down the slope a dozen yards before a forked root halted its progress.

"Now put your face down against the ground and your hands out in front of you; stretch your arms," Grant ordered.

Again Haskins obeyed, shivering; he was pretty well convinced that his last hour had come, and there was nothing he could do about it.

Grant stepped forward a couple of paces. He leaned over and plucked Haskins' Colt from its holster and shoved it under his own belt. For a long moment he stood looking down at the prostrate man. Haskins lay motionless save for a spasmodic shuddering that shook his frame from time to time. Grant drew a heavy knife from its boot sheath. There was a flash of steel.

Haskins screamed. He writhed over on his side, clutching his blood-spurting right hand, the severed index finger of which lay on the pine needles. Grant spoke.

"Guess you'll have to learn to trigger with another finger before you go in for your next killing," he said.

Haskins mouthed and gibbered, his face contorted, his eyes glaring up at Grant.

"I'll kill you!" he screamed, his voice cracking with rage and pain.

Grant turned on his heel and walked back the way he had come. Behind him sounded the reedy, whimpering scream of the mutilated man.

"I'll kill you! I'll kill you!"

Tossing Haskins' Colt aside, Jim Grant walked unhurriedly to where he had left his big moros with the split reins hanging as a warning not to stray. He mounted the blue horse and sent him diagonally south by east through the brush, reaching the trail some distance below the bend. His face was still set, but the wrath which had enveloped him when he had seen Haskins lying there, rifle ready, was cooling and the inevitable reaction was setting in.

With a shrug, he dismissed Haskins and gave his attention to the business at hand. As Joel Collison's range boss and trail boss of the drive, it was his chore to ride ahead and find a suitable bedding-down spot for the Swinging J herd. The sun was low in the west when he found a place he considered satisfactory, a wide clearing with a little stream washing its inner edge. He rode to the creek, got the rig off Smoke, the blue horse, so that he could feed and roll in comfort, had a drink himself and then rolled a cigarette which he smoked with relish. Inhaling deeply, he watched the trail to the north. Already the chuck wagon would have rolled ahead so as to reach the bedding-down spot before the herd put in an appearance and give the cook an opportunity to have supper ready for the hungry cowboys by the time the herd was bedded down.

Half an hour elapsed before the lumbering wagon hove into view, old Joel Collison riding beside it. Pulling into the clearing, the cook quickly unhitched and began hauling out his Dutch ovens and other utensils. Collison dismounted beside the range boss and nodded his approval.

"A good spot," he said.

"In another week, barring bad luck, you'll be bedding down on your own holding," Grant returned.

4

"I hope so," said Collison. "It's been a long drive and a hard one."

Grant nodded. "Would have been shorter if we'd come straight across the Nueces, but I figured it was better to circle north and miss as much of the rough country as we could," he observed. "Pretty bad from here on, and we'll have to take it slow; the cows are tired."

"Figure you were right about the northern route; you know the country," said Collison. "Well, we haven't lost much on the way, and nothing bad has happened so far. Wonder where the devil Haskins got to? Haven't seen him all day. I figured he decided to scout ahead and you'd meet him riding back."

"No, I didn't meet him riding back," Grant replied.

"Wonder where he got to?" Collison repeated.

"I've a notion you won't see Haskins again for a while," Grant answered. He started to tell Collison of his encounter with Haskins, then abruptly decided not to; he didn't feel like talking about the incident, which had left a very bad taste in his mouth.

"Figure he pulled out?" asked Collison.

"I wouldn't be surprised," Grant returned noncommittally.

"Can't say as I would be, either," Collison admitted. "I've a notion he was getting pretty well fed up with the long drive and hankering for a bust in town. Maybe he pulled ahead and made for that town you spoke of being down there to the southwest — Laredo, wasn't it?"

"That's right; Laredo," Grant replied.

"Uh-huh, I bet he did just that," said Collison. "He's been sort of put out ever since I made you range boss when poor Si Perkins got killed. Haskins had had his eye on the job for quite a while. He wouldn't have got it, though, even if you hadn't come along when you did. He's a good puncher, but he doesn't know how to handle men; he'd have had the whole outfit by the ears in a week. Just not the sort to get along with others, and given a bit of authority, he'd have been impossible. Smart enough, all right, and educated. His dad wanted him to be a lawyer, and he did study for it in college and practised for a while before the old man died, and did all right. I recall Judge Dice once saying that Lafe has as fine a legal brain as he had come across in his experience, but no common sense or decency to go with it. Anyhow, Lafe threw it up after his dad passed on. Reckon he was too darned restless to fit into a law office. He went back to range work, along with considerable hell-raising of one kind or another. Had a habit of riding off all of a sudden and not showing up for months, like he did last year. I hired him because his dad, old Westbrook Haskins, was a mighty good friend of mine. Otherwise I wouldn't have done it."

Grant's only comment was a nod.

CHAPTER
TWO

Nearly an hour passed before the marching column of cattle appeared. It was a big herd and a mixed one, made up chiefly of longhorns but with a fair sprinkling of heavier, more stolid improved stock. After the herd and the remuda of spare horses came three covered wagons bearing tools, Joel Collison's household effects and other necessities.

The point men deftly veered the leaders to the right, and soon the cows were drinking and grazing while the cook dished up steaming chuck for the hungry punchers. After eating, the cowboys smoked and told yarns for a while and then rolled up in their blankets, save those chosen for the first trick of night guard. With the weather fine, Grant did not anticipate any trouble with his temperamental four-footed charges, but experience had taught him to take no chances. Longhorns would sometimes stampede for no reason at all, and rounding up several thousand beefs scattered all over the landscape was a chore nobody hankered for.

The following morning, to the accompaniment of noise, orderly confusion and much jovial profanity, the drive got under way, the cows stringing out in a long column and trudging along stolidly.

Hour after hour the great herd trudged on. This was chaparral country, choked with thorny brush. Nature created in this area and to the north and east that breed of cattle found nowhere else on earth — the long-legged, lean-flanked, hard-headed, wild-eyed Texas longhorn. Without the stamina, the endurance and hardihood of this breed, the long trail drives over mountains, deserts, and prairies would have been impossible. They throve where the softer, heavier breeds of the East would have starved.

For the most part, the land was level, but every so often a range of low but rugged hills would start up unexpectedly from the prairie, necessitating a slow and arduous climb on the part of the weary cattle.

Just such a range loomed a few miles ahead when the herd bedded down the evening of the third day after Grant's encounter with Haskins. The trail wound snakily up the slopes to flow into a notch with sloping, brush-grown sides. The notch was narrow, and even with the sun still above the horizon it was shadowy, having the appearance from a distance of the mouth of a cave.

Standing a little apart from the others, Jim Grant eyed that dark cleft with disfavour. They were in outlaw country now, a favourite operating ground for rustlers. Less than forty miles to the south was the Rio Grande, with Mexico and a fine market for "wet" cows beyond. With twenty men guarding the herd, Grant was inclined to discount the possibility of trouble; but the wide-loopers of the land between the Nueces and the Rio Grande were as shrewd as they were salty and might use any sort of unexpected stratagem. And that brush-walled, rugged pass through the hills could provide opportunity for a daring and cunning bunch. He continued to study the pass and the brush-grown slopes on either side.

Abruptly he sensed rather than saw a flicker of movement on the crest of the rise to the west. An instant later his eye caught a sudden quick sparkle that could have been sunlight reflecting from a polished bit iron or the surface of a silver concha on an unseen rider's chaps.

But neither flicker nor glint was repeated, and Grant was inclined to believe both had been figments of an overwrought imagination. Gradually, however, as his gaze drifted back and forth across the climbing wall of chaparral attention focused on something that could be of significance. It was a sort of indenture in the growth, crawling crookedly up the western slope, resembling two poorly trimmed parallel hedgerows.

"What you looking at, Jim?" Joel Collison's voice asked behind him.

"I don't know for sure, Uncle Joel," Grant answered slowly. "I thought I saw something move up there; could have been a horse and rider."

Collison looked serious. "You mean some hellions might be watching us bed down and planning to make a try for our cows tonight?"

Jim Grant shook his head. "Not tonight. Not out here in the open. They could never get away with it. But if some gents of easy conscience happen to be holed up in the brush tomorrow while we're driving through the pass, it could be different. It's narrow in there between the brush, and the boys will have to bunch behind the herd — no room for outriders — and they'd be setting quail for a couple of well directed volleys. They'd be blasted to pieces before they could get into action."

Collison's face assumed worried lines. "You've got me bothered!" He grumbled querulously. "What are we going to do about it?"

"I'll try and figure something," Grant answered. "Let's go eat."

After he finished eating, Grant rolled a cigarette and beckoned the Swinging J hands to gather around him.

In a few terse sentences he recounted what he had seen and what he suspected.

"I may be just a nervous Nelly and imagining things," he concluded, "but I figure we can't afford to take chances."

A chorus of ejaculations arose, most of them profane. Grant waited patiently for the tumult to subside.

"Swearing won't help," he said when something like quiet was restored. "What we've got to do is get the jump on those hellions."

"How you going to do it, Jim?" a hand asked.

"Here's the plan I've worked out," Grant explained. "In the morning, I want the herd to roll on as usual, just as if nothing was suspected. But an hour before daylight I'll take seven men and ride that snake track I'm pretty sure runs up through the brush. If we can get to the top of the hill and drift down it a ways without being seen or heard, we should be able to spot the hellions, if they really are there, and turn the tables on them."

"Makes sense to me," said old Joel. "Count me as one of the seven."

CHAPTER
THREE

Grant was already awake when one of the night hawks touched him on the shoulder. He arose, feeling much refreshed, shook himself and glanced at the sky.

"The boys ready, Pat?" He asked.

"All set," the cowboy replied.

Grant again studied the sky, and shook his head disapprovingly. There was no moon, but a brilliant glitter of stars made visibility disquietingly good. He strode over to where his seven men waited at their horses' heads.

"All right," Grant said, "let's go."

The horses' hoofs making only a soft patter on the heavily grass-grown prairie, the little posse headed for the dark slopes that, in the starlight, had the look of some gigantic crouching monster. Jim Grant never took his eyes off the shadowy crest, watching intently for the telltale shine of shifted metal. However, he saw nothing, and they reached the bottom of the long slope without incident.

There was a trail up the slope, little more than a winding game track, but showing evidence of considerable travel at one time.

After what seemed an eternity of apprehension and suspense, they reached the hilltop and drifted slowly across its few hundred yards of level surface. Grant breathed a little easier as they began the descent of the opposite slope. He reasoned that if an ambush had been planned, the logical spot for it would have been the crest.

They were a third of the way down the winding track to the pass floor when Grant called a halt.

"This is as far as we can take a chance on the horses," he told his followers in a whisper. "From here on it's shanks' mare, and for the love of Pete watch where you put your feet and don't go brushing against the bushes."

"Think they're really here, Jim?" old Joel breathed.

"I've got a hunch they are," Grant replied. "I feel it in my bones."

"The Scotch are supposed to have the second sight, and you've got a lot of Scotch blood," muttered Collison.

"Second sight or no, I feel they're here," Grant answered. "Let's go."

At little better than a crawl the posse eased down the trail. Sunrise was streaking the sky with scarlet and gold and the light was strengthening by the second. But in the depths of the narrow pass the shadows still curdled.

Grant glanced up at the flaming sky. The herd should have been under way for nearly an hour and would be approaching the base of the north slope. He could see now that the track he followed diagonalled down to the floor of the pass, which couldn't be more than a hundred yards distant. He took a few more cautious steps and halted abruptly, his followers jostling to a stop behind him. From the dark depths beneath came a mutter of voices.

"They're there!" He breathed to Collison. "Keep perfectly still till the light strengthens."

Without sound or movement the posse stood waiting. Light was flowing down the slope like water. It reached the floor of the notch, the shadows fled, and objects stood out in clear relief.

Huddled in the brush that fringed the trail through the pass were nearly a dozen men. The light glinted on the barrels of drawn guns.

Grant drew his guns; his followers did likewise. They were close now, within easy range. He whispered an order to halt.

And then the unpredictable happened. A cowhand stepped on a smooth round stone that rolled under his foot. He floundered off balance, grabbed wildly for support and fell, managing to let off his gun in such a manner that the slug passed within an inch of Grant's head.

"Let 'em have it!" Grant roared as the outlaws whirled around with cries of alarm and dived for cover. Instantly the silent growth fairly exploded to a roar of gunfire.

Three of the owlhoots fell, but the others were holed up in the brush and answered the fire with deadly accuracy. A cowboy pitched forward on his face and lay still. Another yelled shrilly as a bullet tore through his shoulder. A slug ploughed a stinging furrow along

Grant's ribs and knocked nearly all the breath from his lungs. He gasped, gulped, but continued to pull trigger as fast as he could.

Outnumbered two to one, the little posse fought desperately, but Grant knew it was a losing battle. He winced as a bullet whistled past his face, coming from a wide angle.

"They're circling around through the brush to surround us," he told Collison. "Looks like we've bit off more than we can chew."

"Maybe," grunted old Joel as he fired at a smoke puff. "What's that racket?"

Grant heard it, too, a steady clicking that quickly became the pound of racing hoofs. The Swinging J hands had circled the herd and were tearing up the slope to the rescue.

"Let 'em have it!" Grant shouted. "Here come the boys!"

The outlaws, too, realized what was happening. A voice shouted an order. There was a crashing of brush, dimly seen figures streaking it down the pass. Grant fired twice, and one of the figures went end over like a plugged rabbit. But before he could pull trigger again, the fleeing men had darted around a clump of brush and out of sight. An instant later fast hoofs clattered south through the pass.

Grant began reloading his guns. Pursuit was out of the question, because they had left the horses far up the trail.

"Stay where you are," he told his men. "One of those hellions may be only wounded and deadly as a broken-backed rattler. Wait till the boys show. Is poor Pat done for?"

"Got him dead centre," growled Collison, "and Wes Lawrence has a hole between his eyes. Anyhow, we got some of them."

The cowboys, crouched in the brush, were performing rude but efficient surgery on their wounded companions — the man with a smashed shoulder and another with a bullet-punctured thigh — when the remainder of the Swinging J outfit stormed into view and jerked their lathered horses to a slithering halt in obedience to Grant's hail.

"First off make sure of those devils on the ground," the range boss ordered. "Four of them; maybe more."

A fifth dead man was discovered in the brush, and spots of blood on the stones indicated that there were wounded among those who had escaped.

"Not too bad — five for two," said Collison.

"Yes, but the two we lost were worth a thousand of those hombres," Grant replied bitterly.

The dead outlaws were hard-looking specimens but with nothing outstanding about them. Typical border brush poppers, Grant decided. He vetoed suggestions of pursuit.

"They've got a head start and they know the country," he explained. "Chances are we couldn't come up with them, and if we did it would be very likely some place where everything would be in their favour. Might as well go back and get the herd rolling."

The hands obeyed, and when the chuck wagon arrived the bodies of the dead cowboys were loaded into it. That evening there were two more low mounds on the prairie south of the hills.

The morning of the third day after the fight in the pass, Grant announced to Joel Collison, "Tonight, if nothing goes wrong, you'll be squatting on your own property."

All day, with a single brief pause at noon, the herd rolled south by west. An hour before sunset the leaders, Grant and Collison riding beside them, topped a long slope and trudged through a notch. Before them lay a wide and shallow valley, well watered, grown with wheat grasses and dotted with groves and thickets.

"There she is," Grant observed as they halted their horses.

"It looks to be all you and Sanchez claimed for it," replied Collison, his gaze appreciating the emerald and amethyst billows of prairie. "What's that smoke way down to the southeast?"

"That's the railroad and the town, Laredo," answered Grant. "Quite a town, too. I stopped there a spell when I rode over from Sanderson."

"And what's that down there by the trees — a reception committee?" remarked Collison, gesturing toward three horsemen who had flashed around the northern straggle of a grove and appeared to be heading for the notch.

"Reckon not," decided Grant as the three riders suddenly wheeled their mounts and went streaking into the southwest. "'Pears they sighted us up here and don't want any part of us."

"Wonder why?" said Collison.

"Reckon there's the reason why," Grant replied, as from the shadow of the grove bulged five more horsemen going like the wind. From their ranks spurted wisps of smoke, like dust from a stepped-on puffball. To the ears of the watchers in the notch came a crackling sound as of thorns burning under a pot.

"Range a bit too far for six-guns," Grant observed, "and it looks like the gents in front are pulling away from them. There they go into the brush. Appears to be some sort of a disagreement. I've a notion this is a nice section, Boss."

"Maybe for young squirts like you, but at my age, I hanker for peace and quiet," Collison grunted. "Oh, well, may have been nothing but some skylarkin'. Here comes the wagon, so we better amble down to the creek over there and get ready to make camp. Tomorrow we'll choose a good spot for a house, and then ride to town and see if we can find some gents to help build it."

CHAPTER
FOUR

At the time of its inception, Laredo had been truly a frontier community. But the advent of two railroads, one from Corpus Cristi in 1880 and the other from Mexico in 1881, put an end to its isolation and opened a large number of Mexican markets to Texas. Soon irrigation would change the arid Rio Grande valley into a garden spot; and already there was a bustling, prosperous atmosphere that hinted at days to come when this important port of entry would handle sixty per cent of all the freight to cross the International Border.

However, when Jim Grant and Joel Collison rode into the pueblo on a pleasant spring afternoon, Laredo was still a "very plain city" whose prevailing style of architecture utilized stone or sun-dried brick walls and thatched roofs.

"The darn place is growing like a mushroom in the dark," Grant declared. "Seems twice as large as when I was here a couple of years back, and the saloons appear to be leading the pack; every other building seems to house one."

"Or a dance hall or gambling joint," added Collison. "Now where'd we best head for to tie onto some labour and building materials?"

"Sheriff's office, I'd say," replied Grant. "Sheriffs know everything; I think he hangs out on Farragut Street and Salinas Avenue."

They located the office without difficulty. The sheriff, a lank old frontiersman with frosty eyes and a drooping moustache, greeted them pleasantly enough.

"Reckon your best bet is Frank Potter's general store right around the next corner on Convent Avenue," he said after Collison had outlined his needs. "Potter deals in building supplies and handles construction matters, and he's okay. Aim to take up land hereabouts?"

"Reckon we've already taken it up," replied Collison. "I bought a holding from a feller here named Camera Sanchez."

The sheriff blinked and stared. "The devil you did!" He exclaimed.

"That's right," nodded Collison. "Bought it last fall; we're from the Nueces country."

"The pastures east of his wire, eh?" muttered the sheriff. "The land he didn't fence."

"Guess that's so," admitted Collison.

The sheriff appeared about to ask another question, then apparently changed his mind.

"Yes, Potter is your best bet," he repeated.

"Okay, and much obliged," Collison said. "We'll go see him."

Outside, he remarked to Grant, "That old lawman seemed sort of surprised to hear we'd bought here."

"Yes, he did," Grant agreed thoughtfully. "Surprised, and something else. I couldn't figure just what, but I had a feeling he didn't approve. I'm of a notion he

20

started to give us some advice and then decided not to. I wonder if there is something down here we didn't learn about."

"Could be," Collison replied indifferently. "Let's go make a deal for building our ranch-house."

Some instinct had caused Camera Sanchez to refrain from confiding his deal with Joel Collison to anybody other than Lila and lanky Jess Sanborn. So the arrival of the Nueces cattlemen came as a surprise to everybody in the section, including the sheriff and Cale Whitmer.

Grant and Collison had no trouble finding the big general store. Frank Potter proved to be a plump and amiable individual who appeared pleased with the chance to do business after old Joel produced credentials, bank statements and references. But when the site chosen for the proposed ranchhouse was mentioned, a startled look crossed his face. He hesitated, tugged at his lower lip and rubbed the sharp bridge of his nose.

"I make a point of getting paid on delivery for all building material," he announced abruptly.

"No objection to that," said Collison.

Jim Grant, however, was of a more critical turn of mind.

"Mr. Potter," he said, "why did you do such a sudden about-face?"

"Sudden about-face!" Repeated the storekeeper.

"Yes," Grant said. "A moment ago you had no intention of asking for immediate payment. Why did you change your mind?"

Frank Potter rubbed his nose again. He hemmed and hawed a moment, and drew a deep breath in the manner of a man who resolves to plunge into a subject he'd rather not discuss.

"Reckon you must have bought from Camera Sanchez," he stated rather than asked.

"That's right," replied Grant. "Anything wrong with Sanchez?"

"Not a thing, not a thing," the storekeeper hastened to assure him. "A fine feller; the Sanchezes have always been fine people. But, you see, the Rafter S has had a mite of trouble with the Whitmer outfit, the Bradded R, over to the west of Camera's holdings, and folks are scared it ain't over yet. Both outfits have got lots of friends who are kinda taking sides."

"I see," nodded Grant. "Trouble of recent origin?"

"Started about five months back, when Sanchez run his wire," said Potter. "I see now why he didn't fence farther to the east. Reckon you must have bought farther back than five months."

"We did, about seven months ago," Grant replied. "And the Sanchez and Whitmer outfits are in a row, with the prospect of something resembling a range war in the making?"

"Guess that's about it," conceded Potter.

"And you figure we, having bought from Sanchez, will probably back his play and be in the middle of the ruckus?"

Potter pulled his lip, rubbed his nose and looked uncomfortable.

"And so," Grant pursued, "you figure you had better play safe and get your money without delay. That about it?"

"Well, guess you've stated the case rather accurate," the storekeeper admitted. "You see, when that sort of trouble busts loose, sometimes in the morning a building, or a half built one, ain't where it was the night before."

"Yes," Grant agreed. "In the course of such a row fire is a weapon not infrequently employed. Very well, Mr. Potter, I think I can speak with Mr. Collison's approval when I tell you that you will receive payment for your materials as soon as delivered, and that the builders you send along can draw their wages at the completion of each day's work, if they are so minded. And if you happen to speak with the Whitmer gent who appears to be on the prod, you might mention to him that we didn't come here looking for trouble, but that we have in our outfit twenty Nueces cowhands who don't take kindly to being pushed around."

The storekeeper regarded him steadfastly a moment; then suddenly he grinned, a grin that made his chubby face very pleasant to look upon.

"Son," he said, "I done changed my mind again. You can pay for your materials in regular fashion, when convenient, and I reckon the boys with the hammers and saws I send out will be satisfied with regular Saturday pay days."

"Thank you, Mr. Potter," Grant said. He and the storekeeper shook hands.

When they reached the street old Joel, who had stood silent during the passage between Grant and the storekeeper, chuckled delightedly.

"Jim, you sure have a way with folks when you start talking to 'em straight from the shoulder," he said. "You made that little gent feel a mite ashamed of himself, I reckon."

"He's a fair man," Grant replied, "and I've a notion that despite his baby face he isn't the sort that would stand for much pushing around."

"Kinda recognized a kindred spirit and approved of you, eh?"

"Perhaps." Grant smiled. "I'm hungry."

"Me, too," said Collison. "Let's go find a bite."

A few minues later they neared a big saloon that featured much plate glass. A sprightly scraping of fiddles and strumming of guitars floated over the swinging doors.

"Looks like a good place," declared Collison. "I like music with my meals. The Montezuma! Named after the street, I reckon; but what the devil was the street named after?"

Grant refrained from explaining, being in no mind for a dissertation on the martyred Aztec emperor. Old Joel forgot all about it and gazed around complacently as they took a table near the dance floor.

The Montezuma was a busy place, all right. Three roulette wheels were whirring; there were a number of poker tables going full blast, a chuck-a-luck game and a faro bank. Quite a few couples occupied the dance floor, and the long bar was well crowded.

"The gals ain't bad, either," Collison stated.

"Fair to middling dance floor *señoritas*, but as you said, not bad," Grant conceded cheerfully. "Let's eat."

They did, with appetite. The Montezuma's food, like the dance floor girls, wasn't bad. Afterward they ordered drinks. Grant was leaning back comfortably in his chair, rolling a cigarette, when he saw the girl.

She had just come from the dressing room and was standing at the edge of the dance floor with the other girls, the orchestra having taken time out for a drink. Her hair was flame-coloured and abundant. Grant could not be sure whether her big eyes were black or green.

Altogether, he thought, she stood out from her companions like a stately rose amid a clump of cheerful daisies. Abruptly he realized he was staring almost rudely. He shifted his gaze and saw the man.

He was a big man, rather good-looking, Grant thought, with a big-featured, bad-tempered face, a mane of tawny hair and intolerant dark eyes. Those eyes were at the moment fixed on the girl, and there was a hot glow of anger in their depths.

The orchestra struck up a lively tune. A gay young cowhand stepped up to the girl and spoke to her. She nodded noncommittally, the puncher encircled her slender waist with a long arm, and they danced.

She was graceful as a flower swaying in the dawn wind, her movements rhythmical perfection, and when she smiled at her partner, her teeth flashed white and even against her red lips.

Old Joel chuckled under his moustache. "And she ain't bad, either," he remarked. "Fact is, I'd say she's a little better than not bad, eh, Jim?"

"What the devil is a girl like that doing dancing in a place like this?" Grant replied.

Old Joel shrugged. "Maybe she likes to eat," he hazarded. "Nothing wrong with honest work of any kind, son, and it strikes me this place is strictly on the up-and-up. So why shouldn't a girl make an honest living dancing in here?"

Grant didn't have an answer for that one, but just the same he had a feeling she didn't 'belong'.

His glance shifted to the man standing a little distance from the dance floor. His hot anger of a moment before seemed to have cooled a little, but was replaced by a vindictiveness that made the hard lines of his face even harder. The man abruptly turned, walked to the bar and ordered a drink. He downed it at a gulp and ordered another.

The girl sauntered across the room. When she reached Grant's table she paused and smiled.

"May I have this one?" he asked.

"Of course," she answered. "That's what I'm here for."

Grant was slightly taken aback at the unexpected reply, but he encircled her waist and they glided across the floor. Grant was a good dancer and he liked to dance, and in this red-haired girl with the eyes he now definitely decided were green, he found a satisfactory partner.

Old Joel chuckled as he watched them, and sighed, "Oh, to be fifty again!"

The number was a lively one, and when the music ceased the girl was a bit breathless.

"Hope my awkwardness didn't tire you," Grant said.

"Quite the contrary," she answered. "You are very light on your feet for a big man. I really enjoyed it."

"Shall I buy a drink?" he asked.

"Not just at present, if you don't mind," she declined. "After another number or two; I'd much prefer to sit at the table with you and that nice-looking old gentleman. I don't drink much."

"Your complexion attests to that," he complimented her.

She smiled a little and returned a joking reply.

Grant was surprised and a bit intrigued at her diction and choice of words. More than ever he was convinced that she didn't 'belong'.

Suddenly her eyes darkened the merest trifle and her breath caught in her throat; she was staring over his shoulder toward the bar.

Grant turned his head slightly and saw the big man he had noted watching the girl striding toward them, his face convulsed with anger. A pace distant he paused, ignoring Grant, his eyes glowering at the girl.

"Norma, this is too much!" he growled. "Everybody's talking, and you're making me look ridiculous. Get out of here and go home."

"I have no home, and I'm staying here," she replied coolly.

"And I say you're not!" he blazed at her.

"Cale, I'm past twenty-one," she answered meaningly.

The man Cale rasped something that sounded like an oath, and his great paw shot out and gripped her shoulder.

"Cale, leave me alone," she said, her voice still cool. His grip tightened, and she winced a little. Then slim steely fingers coiled about his big wrist — and Cale's hand opened convulsively, freeing the girl. Grant slammed it down against his side.

"Better do as the lady says," he said.

Cale glared at him, his hand reaching for the butt of the big gun swung low against his thigh. Grant stood perfectly still, his hands hanging loose, waiting.

The other hesitated, the rage in his eyes replaced by a speculative look. He slowly shook his head.

"Nope, I wouldn't have a chance," he said. "I know a quick-draw two-gun man when I see one, and I ain't that sort. But, feller, if you'll shuck off those belts, I'll shuck off mine and give you the trimming of your life."

As Grant hesitated, the girl broke in. "Why do you always have to be an uncouth bore, Cale?" she demanded hotly. "Besides, you're twice as big as he is; you're just taking advantage of his size."

That did it! Grant unbuckled his belts, handed them to Joel Collison who stood to one side, his watchful eyes shooting glances around the crowded room that had suddenly hushed in expectancy. Cale tossed his to a grinning cowhand.

"Clear the floor and give us room," he growled.

"And no interference from *anybody*, gents," old Joel said significantly, a thumb hooked over his cartridge belt close to his holster.

The floor was quickly cleared and ringed about by a dense crowd. The two men squared away, and the fight was on.

Cale rushed, his great fists flailing. Grant met him with a left and right that rocked him back on his heels. He recovered, rushed again. They closed, slugging it out toe to toe. Grant gave ground before his much heavier opponent and danced away. Cale followed, growling and muttering. Neither had much scientific knowledge of the art of self-defence; it was largely hit and be hit, with power behind the blows. They closed again. A wild flurry of blows followed, and Grant was beaten to his knees. He surged erect before Cale could leap in for the kill, a taste of sulphur in his mouth, his head spinning. Both men were bleeding freely now. Grant had a deep cut in his right cheek, another over his left eye. Cale's nose was streaming, blood dribbling from his split lips. His teeth, showing in a wolfish grin, were reddened. He came thundering in once more, caught Grant with a sizzling left on his cut cheek, and the blood spurted. Grant countered with a blow that laid Cale's chin open to the bone. Both were breathing in hoarse gasps, their bloody faces contorted with pain and effort. Now they were grimly silent, saving every ounce of energy for the battle.

As Grant had suspected, he was much the quicker. He hit Cale three times to Cale's once, but Cale's blows had three times the force of his; his forearms were bruised to either elbow, his ribs sore and aching. The blood streaming from his cut brow got into his eyes and at times half blinded him. He fought desperately, savagely, now, taking advantage of every opening, knowing that his strength was ebbing.

Cale's fighting stance was peculiar. He stood with his big shoulders stooped somewhat forward, his right arm drawn back, his left flung across his chest; and although he struck oftener with his right, Grant watched that big left fist and knotted forearm, for it was in that passive left he believed his danger lay.

They closed again, and Grant took a terrific pounding from Cale's jabbing, slashing right, and knew he couldn't take much more; he still watched that deadly left that Cale used so seldom. And presently it came, with arm and shoulder and body behind it — quick as a flash and irresistible as a cannon ball.

But Grant was ready. He leaped aside and struck, and caught Cale clean and true upon the angle of the jaw. Spinning around, Cale fell and lay with his bloody face buried in the sawdust. He was hideous with blood and sweat, bruised and cut and disfigured, and Jim Grant was in little better condition. The difference was, Cale was out cold, while Grant was still on his feet, stumbling and weaving but erect.

As he tottered, breathing hoarsely, he realized an arm was around him, steadying him, supporting him till his strength returned; a slender, rounded arm that nevertheless was surprisingly strong. The girl by his side spoke, her voice thrilling.

"Some man!"

CHAPTER
FIVE

The portly owner of the Montezuma shouldered his way through the jabbering crowd, a couple of swampers at his heels.

"Take him into the back room and throw some water over him and he'll come to after a bit," he ordered, gesturing to Cale's prostrate form. "Take his gun along with him."

"You don't have to worry, feller," he told Grant as Cale was borne away. "Cale's an ugly customer — he'll hate you and hold a grudge — but he ain't the sort to shoot a man in the back."

Grant nodded, buckling on his own belts; he had already formed some such opinion of his opponent. He swabbed his face with a blood-drenched handkerchief and began to feel somewhat better.

A man who had just entered the saloon pushed his way to the front; an exceedingly handsome man with yellow hair and deeply blue eyes. Grant recognized Camera Sanchez.

The recognition was mutual. "Why, hello, Mr. Collison; so you finally got here," Sanchez greeted him. "Hello, Grant, what the devil did you do — run into a barn?"

"Sort of," Grant admitted smiling with difficulty because of his gashed and swollen lips.

"The *barn* was just carried out," chuckled old Joel.

"Who were you fighting with, Grant?" Sanchez asked.

"It was Cale Whitmer!" an excited voice exclaimed at his elbow. "This feller knocked him cold."

Sanchez whistled through his teeth. "Cale Whitmer!" he repeated. "So you had trouble with him first thing. What —" His voice suddenly trailed off. Grant saw he was staring at the red-haired girl, who had moved back a few paces and stood in an attitude of listening.

The girl met his gaze coolly, turned and walked away. Sanchez recovered himself, then turned to Collison and Grant.

"Come on and sit down and have a drink," he invited. "I've a notion Grant can stand a chair under him about now. Here's another handkerchief, Grant, to wipe off the rest of the blood; I don't think you're hurt much."

"Just scratches," Grant replied as they sat down.

"That one on your cheek is one heckuva scratch," grunted Collison. "Who was the good looking red-haired gal, Sanchez? She looked all right."

"She is," Sanchez answered shortly. "Her name's Norma Whitmer and she's Cale Whitmer's cousin. Old Silas, Cale's father, brought her up, but she and Cale don't get along. The other day, or so I heard, they had a devil of a row, and Norma vowed she was going to leave the Bradded R and go to work; looks like she did.

People are talking, of course, and very likely Cale is furious."

"He did 'pear a mite put out about something," old Joel commented.

"I imagine he did," Sanchez said dryly. "What was the fight about, Grant?"

Collison told him. Sanchez shook his head. "It may have been fortunate for Cale, at that, you interfering," he told Grant. "Very likely in another minute she'd have stuck a knife in him. She's a nice girl, but a wildcat when aroused."

"Reckon she ain't got that red hair for nothing," observed old Joel.

Sanchez deftly changed the subject. "I'm afraid you've made a bad enemy, though, Grant," he said. "Whitmer won't forget, and I guess he never forgives."

Grant's glance shifted as Norma came gliding past in the arms of a fat and jolly looking cowhand. She was gazing out the window, over her squat partner's shoulder. Suddenly Grant saw her eyes dilate with a look of horror.

It was her scream of warning that saved him. Even before he saw the gun barrel shoved across the window sill, he was going sideways from his chair. The gun blazed A bullet thudded into the back of the chair he had occupied an instant before.

Grant leaped to his feet, a gun in each hand, and bounded forward, sending a stream of lead hissing through the window. When he reached it, his ears ringing from the bellow of his guns, he thought he heard a patter of feet running down the alley. He fired two shots in the direction of the sound, but with little hope of hitting anything.

The room was in an uproar; men were shouting and cursing, girls screeching. Everybody seemed to be howling questions at once. Grant heard Camera Sanchez exclaim:

"I'd never have believed Cale Whitmer would do a thing like that!"

"You don't know it was Whitmer," Grant told him sharply.

"No, I don't *know* it was Whitmer," Sanchez returned in a voice that left little doubt as to what he believed.

Grant was silent. He glanced about in search of Norma Whitmer but failed to find her. He ejected the spent shells from his guns and replaced them with fresh cartridges. Then he sat down again, after inserting a tentative fingertip into the bullet hole in the back of the chair, and began rolling a cigarette.

"What do you think, Jim?" old Joel asked.

"I don't know," Grant admitted frankly.

He really didn't know what to think, but he noticed something apparently overlooked by everyone else. The way Cale Whitmer wore his holster and the way he fought indicated that he was left-handed, and Grant knew, from the position of the gun barrel across the window sill, that only a left hand could have pulled the trigger.

Camera Sanchez bent a searching glance over the dance floor, shrugged his shoulders and looked at the clock behind the bar.

34

"It's late, and I'll have to be getting back to the spread," he said. "Drop in and see me as soon as you find the time, Mr. Collison. You too, Grant; I figure we should get better acquainted. A place to sleep? The Great Western Hotel across the street is as good as any. Hope you feel better in the morning, Grant." With a smile and a nod, he sauntered out.

Old Joel watched him go, tugged his moustache and remarked.

"A nice feller, all right, Jim, and even though it looks like we've dropped spang in the middle of a first class row, I still believe it was a good move."

"I believe so, too," Grant said, and meant it. "Let's go to bed."

CHAPTER SIX

As Grant had shrewdly surmised he would do, Lafe Haskins did circle the Swinging J herd and ride straight for Laredo.

Reaching Laredo in the deepening dusk, Haskins headed for a big waterfront saloon of dubious character near the International Bridge, which was run by Garland Shane, also known as Whispering Shane, also sometimes known as The Spider. He was ushered into a back room where Whispering Shane was propped up in bed, for Mr. Shane did most of his sleeping in the daytime.

Power chooses odd houses for itself. The saloon owner was no full-blooded, overbearing ruffian with a gun at his hip and a knife in his boot top. Whispering Shane was a thin, sallow little man with iron-grey hair and a wiry mustache; he would have fitted very well behind his own lunch counter in a dirty apron. Only his eyes belied him; they had the hard glitter of a nocturnal animal that prowls the hours of darkness on stealthy pads.

Nothing ever surprised Whispering Shane. He had not seen Haskins for several months, but he greeted the haggard, wild-eyed man with the blood-caked bandage around his hand as if Haskins had just dropped in to pass the time of day after spending the preceding evening in his company.

"Howdy, Haskins," he said in the soft, almost inaudible voice that gave him his name. "Have a chair; I'll send for a drink."

Haskins dropped into the chair, his mouth working. Whispering Shane lolled back on his pillows, his eyes dull opaque. He reached out and pulled a bell cord. A moment later a waiter, apparently inspired, entered the room with a tray on which were two glasses and a bottle of whiskey. Without speaking, he placed the tray on a chair within Shane's reach and retired.

Whispering Shane took the bottle in a thin blue-veined hand and filled the glasses to the brim. He passed one to Haskins, who took it clumsily in his left hand and swallowed it at a gulp, a few drops of the liquor dribbling down his chin. Shane silently refilled the glass.

The second followed the first. Shane refilled the glass again.

Abruptly his eyes flamed. "All right," he said, "talk!"

Haskins swallowed half the third glass. He hiccoughed, wiped his lips with his dirty shirt-sleeve and fumbled tobacco and paper from his pocket. Shane watched the operation in silence. Haskins got the cigarette going and leaned forward, his face working and twisting.

"Shane," he said, "I'm going to kill a man."

Shane was not impressed. "Won't be the first, I gather," he replied.

"Yes, I'm going to kill him," Haskins repeated, "and I'm going to make a beggar of another."

"Laudable ambitions, doubtless, from your point of view," Shane commented. "Suppose you tell me what set you off."

Haskins told him, his voice choking with anger, his remarks liberally interspersed with curses. Shane listened in silence, his eyes opaque, his face expressionless.

"Grant should have killed you, and I wonder why he didn't," he observed as Haskins paused, breathing as if he had just finished running a race. "Guess he just isn't the killer type," Shane added reflectively. "Better be careful, though, or you'll make him one; I've seen it happen before."

"I'll make him buzzard bait!" Haskins declared.

"Maybe," Shane conceded without conviction. "And you hold that Collison did you wrong, too, eh? I can't see it. Incidentally, I'm not interested in killing or beggaring people. Why did you come to me?"

"Because I'll need help to accomplish what I have in mind."

"Naturally; otherwise you wouldn't have come." Shane nodded. "But where do I come in on this plan you claim to have up your sleeve? I repeat, I'm not interested in killings or beggarings. What have you got to interest me?"

"Among other things, there are nearly ten thousand head of cattle heading this way from the Nueces," Haskins said.

"A big herd," Shane remarked. "So you think there's a chance to drop a loop on it?"

"I do," Haskins replied. "It's sure worth trying."

"Yes, it's worth trying," Shane said slowly. "All right, I'll send word to the boys to come in pronto, and try not to bungle it; we'll go over the details when they arrive. It's got to be handled shrewdly; I've a notion that the Jim Grant you spoke of is not an easy man to fool."

"I'll fool him, damn him!" Haskins declared venomously.

"Your hatred for Grant is a weakness in such an affair," Shane said. "Don't allow it to cause you to do some fool thing in your eagerness to get Grant. And now about the other matter, let's hear it."

Haskins hitched his chair a little nearer the bed and spoke in tones as low as Whispering Shane's soft accents. The saloonkeeper listened without comment until Haskins had finished.

"I don't know," he said reflectively. "It's a big order, and we'll be going up against a hard man. Camera Sanchez is a cold proposition. I'd say, though, that he and your *amigos* Grant and Collison also have a weakness — they're law-abiding and wouldn't buck a court decision. But how am I to know you've got your facts straight?"

"Listen, Shane," Haskins said. "I'm a lawyer. I never worked at it much, I'll admit, but I took my degree. I know what I'm talking about. As soon as I heard of this deal between Sanchez and Collison, and listened to what Grant had learned of conditions here, I got interested. Slipped away and did a little investigating on my own hook. There is no record of that old Spanish grant at the land office."

"Nothing so unusual about that," said Shane. "Sanchez must have it, and he'll pull it on us, and then where'll we be?"

"He won't," Haskins stated positively. "Why? Because he hasn't got it, although he thinks he has."

"How do you know he hasn't got it?"

"You'll remember," Haskins said, "that I rode for Sanchez when I was down here the last time, several months back. His hands have the run of the place, and he has no secrets from them. It wasn't hard to learn all about the grant and where it was kept, in an antique strongbox off the living room. It isn't there any more."

"I see," Shane said thoughtfully. His eyes held grudging admiration.

"But," he added, "the original grant is not always necessary to prove ownership. Texas authorities take a broader view of such matters than does the Federal land office and the Court of Claims. Corroborative evidence that the grant was actually ordered and carried out is often considered sufficient to verify the claim, and Texas proceedings are more informal than those of a court of law."

This, as Haskins well knew, was true. Texas, unique among the states, owned its public lands, and land disputes were settled by the Texas courts, the land office or the legislature.

"I'll guarantee that he cannot produce corroborative evidence other than the fact that he and his ancestors occupied the land," Haskins answered.

"Good enough," said Shane, "but if we win the case the land will be ruled state land and for sale, and Sanchez will be granted priority as a buyer."

Haskins smiled craftily. "Agreed," he said. "But it takes money to buy land, and Sanchez hasn't got it. He's land and cattle poor. He used the money he got for the land he sold Collison to buy wire, and he had to borrow more from the bank to finish financing the deal. He's mortgaged heavy. And when things break, the bank will be glad to sell that mortgage if somebody makes an offer for it. That's your angle. Mine is to see to it that Sanchez hasn't anything on which to raise money, although I don't think he could raise anything like what he would need if he sold every cow he owns. When the time comes, he won't have so many to sell, even if he's still alive. I've a notion Whitmer may come in handy in more ways than one, before all's done. Collison will find himself in the same fix; he's just about cleaned out of ready cash and *he* won't be able to raise enough to buy that land a second time. Now what do you think?"

Shane nodded, his eyes brooding. "Maybe it's worth trying," he conceded.

"It is," Haskins declared, and applied a clincher that showed he had vision.

"And that land, or a large part of it, including much of the portion Collison will occupy, in a few years will be worth ten times what it is now. Irrigation is coming to the Rio Grande Valley, and that's all that's needed to make a garden spot of this section. Farmers will vie with one another for a chance to buy."

A strange purplish light flared in Whispering Shane's eyes.

"Yes, maybe it's worth trying," he said. "I'll think about it. Now get out of here; I've got to dress and start work. Go see a doctor and have that hand looked after; you'll be lucky if you don't develop blood poisoning, from the looks of it. Incidentally, you'd better keep out of Sanchez' sight; he might remember you."

"I've already got a fair crop of whiskers started," Haskins replied, rasping the stubble on his chin. "Another week and I'll look a lot different from what I did when I worked for him. And after all, I was just another cowpoke he put on during the busy season. Chances are he never gave me a second look."

Shane nodded. "Be back here about daylight and talk with the boys," he directed.

"Okay," answered Haskins. "I've already figured the spot where we'll make the try for the cows, and we have time to get there before the herd shows."

"And don't let Grant put one over on you again," warned Shane.

Haskins snarled an oath, and his face twisted. Shane paid no attention to his surge of anger.

"Get going," he said, and swung his bare legs over the edge of the bed. "Yes, I'll see Whitmer."

CHAPTER
SEVEN

The workers Frank Potter provided for Grant knew their business, and the materials were plentiful and of the best. Before a week had passed Joel Collison had a roof over his head; the carpenters were putting the finishing touches to the building and were almost ready to start work on the bunkhouse and a commodious barn. The Swinging J punchers, who were fully conversant with such matters, attended to the horse corral themselves.

"Well, I'll be just about busted, so far as ready cash is concerned, but she's worth it," old Joel declared. "All set to spend the rest of my years comfortable."

Things did have a prosperous and contented look. The cattle were scattering and feeding steadily; already they were putting on flesh. The cowboys were getting the lay of the land and were unanimous in their approval of the holding.

Grant also did considerable riding. He learned, among other things, that to the south the valley narrowed, the hills sweeping around in a great curve to the east and south until they almost reached the north bank of the Rio Grande.

From the crest of the hills the country was spread before his eyes like a map; he could see clear across Collison's holdings to where the horizon closed down on the vast acreage of Camera Sanchez' Rafter S, with Cale Whitmer's Bradded R spread beyond.

Camera Sanchez had twice visited the scene of building operations and chatted with Grant and old Joel. However, he had not once mentioned Norma. He was at the ranch house when Grant arrived there, shortly after dark, after a day spent riding the range, and this time he did speak of Cale Whitmer.

"I think you hurt his pride terribly," he told Grant. "He hasn't been seen in the Montezuma since the night you whipped him. I heard he's been hanging out in a rum hole on the waterfront near the International Bridge, a place run by a character known as Whispering Shane, who has a hand in local politics and has been suspected of activities that are dubious, to put it mildly. Appears he and Whitmer have become quite chummy. I wonder why."

"Hard to tell," grunted Collison. "I've a notion we'll find out, however, and it will be something unpleasant. You can expect anything of a hellion who will take a shot at a man through a dark window."

"Uncle Joel, there is no proof it was Whitmer who fired that shot," Grant reminded him.

"Maybe not, but I got my notions," Collison growled. "What do you think, Sanchez?"

Camera hesitated. "I really don't know what to think. It does seem utterly out of character for Whitmer, but you never can tell what a man will do when he's in a

44

blind rage over something. Anyhow, my advice, Jim, is to be on the lookout for Cale Whitmer."

Grant nodded without speaking; he had already resolved to do just that.

CHAPTER
EIGHT

Shane did not need to be told that Haskins had failed to corral the big Swinging J herd; one look at his contorted face was enough.

"So you bungled it," Shane remarked.

"Listen, Shane," Haskins answered, his big hands opening and closing, "I'm in no mood to be taken over the coals."

Shane said nothing, but the queer feral light was in his eyes as he looked at Haskins. He said nothing, just looked, and that look seemed to take all the manhood out of Haskins.

"I'm sorry, Shane," he mumbled, "but every time I think of what happened I see red. I'm beginning to believe Grant isn't a man but a devil. We thought we were laying for him, but it turned out he was laying for us. How he figured out what we had in mind is beyond me, but he did. I'll tell you just what happened and let you decide if the thing wasn't planned perfectly."

He proceeded to do so. Shane listened without comment until he had finished.

Whispering Shane never wasted time in useless recriminations. When the tool with which he worked failed him, he accepted that failure and tried to guard against a repetition. Nothing was to be gained by rehashing the matter.

"Yes, it appears the business was well planned and should have succeeded," he said. "I have only one fault to find with you, and that is that you continue to underestimate Grant. He's as shrewd as he is salty. We lost a chance to turn a nice profit, but there's nothing to be gained by bewailing it. Give your attention to the other angles we discussed. I believe we have something there of more value than Collison's trail herd."

"You've seen Whitmer?" Haskins asked.

"Yes, I've seen him," Shane replied. "He's a bit hesitant, but I think he'll come around to our way of thinking. I've pointed out to him that what we contemplate will be strictly legal, that he will have nothing to worry about and plenty to gain. Also, he hates Camera Sanchez as you hate Grant. A weakness on the part of both of you. Hating is just a waste of time."

"I wonder how you'd feel if Grant had cut off *your* trigger finger," Haskins growled.

"I'd learn to use another finger," Shane answered dryly.

"I'm trying to do just that," Haskins said, scowling blackly. "But it isn't easy, and I'm not much good at gun-slinging with my left hand."

"Then don't use it," Shane counselled. "And try and cool down about Grant. As I said, hating is just a waste of time; I never hate anybody. When somebody gets in my way, I remove him, if I can. Now, forget about

Grant for the time being. I'll take care of him. You say you lost five men in your brush with Grant?"

"That's right: five good men," said Haskins. Shane's lips twisted in a derisive smile.

"Figure they were all done for, none in shape to talk?" he asked.

"That's my opinion," said Haskins. "They sure looked it."

"Now get out of here and get busy," Shane said. "It's up to you to do the spadework before we make our important move. Take my advice and forget your hatred for Grant."

"All right, I will," Haskins promised as he headed for the door. Whispering Shane did not believe him. He halted Haskins with an imperative gesture.

"Haskins," he said, spacing his words, "I repeat, forget about Grant and leave him to me. I'll see to it that he is taken care of properly. Don't forget, Haskins — leave Grant to me!"

CHAPTER
NINE

Jim Grant rode to Laredo the day after his talk with Camera Sanchez.

In front of a well lighted *cantina* he tied Smoke to a convenient rack and entered. The place was crowded, mostly with Mexicans, but there was a fair sprinkling of Texas cowboys who, like himself, had crossed the bridge in search of diversion.

The crowd was lively, the music good, and Grant was served a glass of really excellent wine. He sipped his drink and glanced around with approval. He concentrated his attention on the men drinking at the bar, especially the cowhands from north of the river. He reasoned they represented a good cross-section of the punchers with whom he would be associated from now on.

One man instantly attracted and held his attention. He was a huge young fellow with bristling red hair, snapping brown eyes and a freckled, pug-nosed face. Great freckled hands dangled loosely from long, gorilla-like arms, and his thick shoulders were slightly bowed. In build, he rather reminded Grant of Lafe Haskins. There, however, the resemblance ended. Haskins' bad-tempered features always wore a scowl, while this man's face radiated cheerful good humour. But Grant had a feeling that beneath the puckish exterior was a capacity for furious wrath.

The big fellow caught his eye, raised his glass and drank to him with a flash of crooked but very white teeth.

"Hi, Texas!" He boomed. "Mind if I come over with you?"

The grin was infectious, and Grant smiled in return. "Not at all," he replied, "come along."

The other strode down the bar, walking very lightly for so big a man. He paused, and grinned again.

"My name's Crowley, Zeke Crowley, and I'm from Montana," he announced.

Grant supplied his own name and they shook hands. Crowley's great paw engulfed the Texan's slender hand, but when their hands fell apart, he uttered an exclamation.

"Feller, you got some grip in those fingers," he said, rubbing his own. "I always shake hands hard, and sometimes fellers complain I squeeze a mite too much — though I don't mean no harm by it — but I didn't get nowhere squeezin' with you."

Grant laughed, and changed the subject.

"Montana, I believe you said," he remarked. "You're a long ways from home."

"Oh, I get around," Crowley returned airily. "Been most every place, one time or another. Been hanging around here for a spell. Hafta tie up with some outfit 'fore long now, though. Was figuring to ride back across the bridge tomorrow and look things over. You new down here?"

"Sort of," Grant admitted. "My outfit rolled down from the Nueces country a couple of weeks back."

"Been there," said Crowley. "Dry and thorny. Better down here in the Rio Grande Valley. More water, and a jigger don't even have to wear chaps as a general thing, except in the hills to the north and west; they're plenty rugged. Another thing they got the Nueces country beat on, too. The Nueces specimens ain't no bums, but down here they got the smartest cow thieves in Texas or any place else."

"I'm inclined to agree with you, judging from what I've seen of them," Grant answered.

"How's that?" asked Crowley. "You had a run-in with 'em?"

Grant briefly related his encounter with the raiders in the notch to the north of the valley. Crowley nodded his red head.

"Yep, plumb smart and plumb snake-blooded," he said. "Kill you quick as look at you."

His eyes grew thoughtful. "Feller," he said, "I sort of got a hunch you'd better keep your eyes open; if those hellions figure it was you outsmarted them, they may take a notion to try and even up the score."

"Not beyond the realm of possibility," Grant conceded.

"Got a notion you'll be able to look after yourself, though," Crowley predicted cheerfully. "Say, this place ain't bad, but I know a better one, over to the west a piece, close to the river. What say we get our nags —

mine's hitched right across the street — and amble over there?"

Grant offered no objection, so they secured their horses and rode west almost to where the railroad crossed the river and continued south to Mexico City. Here there were not many buildings, and the lighting was poor. Crowley jerked his thumb toward the trail they were riding.

"Curves around the bend and runs north along the river bank," he announced. "Something interesting up there — remind me to tell you about it later. When I squat for a spell in a new section, I always try to learn all I can about it. Never can tell; it might come in handy sometime."

At a word from Crowley, they pulled up in front of a low building from which came gleams of light and the sounds of boisterous revelry. A long hitchrack accommodated a number of saddled and bridled horses. Grant's keen eyes noted quite a few rifles in saddle boots. Evidently the frequenters of the establishment were in the habit of going well heeled. Some of the horses bore Texas brands; others were "skillet of snakes," Mexican burns not easy to decipher.

They dismounted and left their horses at the rack. Grant noticed that Crowley tethered his mount with a "slip" knot that could be loosened almost instantly. Taking the hint, he merely let the split reins fall to the ground, knowing that Smoke would remain right where he was so long as the straps dangled.

These matters taken care of, they entered the building, which proved to be a well crowded *cantina* rather poorly lighted by two hanging lamps. The air was thick with smoke and aquiver with noise; and everybody appeared to be having a good time.

A Mexican bartender greeted Crowley cordially and included Grant in his friendly smile and nod.

"Wine?" asked Crowley, Grant nodded.

"Funny, ain't it?" chuckled the Montana cowboy. "Other side of the river I always drink whiskey, but down here wine seems the right thing. Well, it's got as much wallop as redeye if you drink enough."

He chuckled again and raised his brimming glass. The wine, ruby-coloured and sparkling, with a fragrant bouquet, was excellent, Grant thought. He sipped from his glass, and his gaze roved over the crowded room.

"Told you it would be lively," said Crowley, adding in a lower tone, "Good to keep your eyes open. Sometimes trouble starts mighty fast. Some tough hombres come in here."

Grant was inclined to agree. While everybody appeared to be on excellent terms with everybody else, there was little doubt but that there were some hard characters present, both American and Mexican. He had a notion, however, that so long as a man attended to his own business he had little to worry about.

Zeke Crowley seemed to know everybody. Soon he was circulating through the crowd, pausing for a word with this one or that, passing jokes with the orchestra. Finally he came back with a svelte little *señorita* with laughing eyes, hair as black as bitumen and vividly red lips.

"This is Teresa," he announced. "She's some gal! I want you to know her, Jim, and dance with her. Can she hoof it!"

Grant's amusement increased, but he didn't deny that the girl was pretty and appeared amiable.

"The tall señor weel dance weeth Teresa?" she asked in halting English, her voice rich and throaty.

Jim Grant was fairly conversant with the Spanish language, and he accepted the invitation courteously in that tongue.

The girl's eyes widened a little. "You do not speak my language as usually do the riders from the North," she said as his arm encircled her slender waist.

Grant did not deem it necessary to mention that he had studied Spanish in college. He merely smiled, and paid her a compliment in the flowery phrases of the land of mañana.

She was a good dancer and companionable, but Grant was not paying her the attention she deserved.

His eyes roved over the room. Nobody seemed to be paying the least attention to him or his dancing partner. Zeke Crowley was at the far end of the bar, laughing and talking with a couple of cowhands and a Mexican or two.

The dance ended. Grant steered Teresa to a nearby table and ordered wine.

"I want to see my amigo at the end of the bar a minute," he told her, and turned to cross the vacated dance floor.

He had taken but a couple of steps when the double doors swung open and three men walked through to pause just inside the entrance, their eyes sweeping the room as if in search of someone. In a swift glance, Grant noted that two were short and squat, the other tall and gangling.

He saw the three pairs of eyes centre on him, saw the men to right and left fan out from the man in the centre.

Jim knew exactly what that meant, and he was going for his guns before the three hands flickered down in a darting movement. The hanging lamps jumped and jangled to the roar of six-shooters.

The man on the right reeled, folded up like a sack of old clothes and fell, his face a horrible crimson mask of torn flesh and spurting blood; a slug had caught him at an angle, smashing his features to shreds.

The man in the centre, the tall one, lurched back as if struck by a mighty fist, but continued to pull trigger. A terrific blow on his left arm knocked Grant almost off balance and he knew he was hit; but the arm was still functioning and he kept blazing away through the fog of powder-smoke.

The tall man suddenly let his gun fall to the floor, sliding from a hand that abruptly seemed utterly weary; he crumpled up on top of it. The third man set himself and took deliberate aim as the hammers of Grant's guns clicked on empty cartridges; his eyes flashed with triumph.

A gun boomed over Grant's shoulder, so close that the powder flame scorched his cheek. The third gunman leaped high in the air with a bubbling shriek, his hands clutching wildly, as if vainly seeking to grasp his escaping soul. Blood gushed from his torn throat and he fell, to lie twitching spasmodically.

The room became a pandemonium of men diving wildly in every direction to get out of line of the flying lead. The dance floor girls were shrieking, the bartenders howling protest. A thrown chair whizzed past Grant's head and crashed into the back bar, bringing down an avalanche of breaking bottles. A gun cracked across the room, and the back bar mirror flew to pieces. Grant saw the gleam of a knife lunging toward him. He threw up one empty gun to deflect the blow, and the steel barely grazed his already wounded left arm. He lashed out with his other gun and missed. The knife sparkled toward him again.

CHAPTER
TEN

A stentorian roar sounded close to Grant. A great hand seized the knife wielder by the neck, jerked him off the floor, whirled him around and around and let go. He shot through the air as if he had taken wings and crashed into three men who were leaping across the open space toward Grant. Zeke Crowley seized a second man and sent him hurtling after the first. Then his right hand tipped up the barrel of the gun he held. Flame gushed from the muzzle, and one of the hanging lamps went out to an accompaniment of screeching metal and tinkling glass. A second shot, the second lamp flew to pieces, and darkness blanketed the room.

Crowley's huge hand closed on Grant's arm. "Straight ahead!" rumbled the Montana puncher. "Side door — I know where it is — hit everything you come to!" He propelled Grant forward, rushing him through the howling, screeching bedlam. Grant dutifully lashed out with his right-hand gun, heard the barrel crunch on flesh and bone. Something warm spurted over his hand; then his arm was jarred to the shoulder as the flailing gun went home a second time.

Crowley could apparently see in the dark. He rushed Grant forward over broken chairs and smashed tables, through the swirling crowd that appeared to have gone completely insane. Guns were booming in every direction, the orange flashes spurting through the murk, blows thudding, yells of pain knifing through the whirl of curses.

They slammed into an obstruction that gave under the impact. A door flew open, and they were in the cool night air with the stars glittering overhead. Crowley continued to propel Grant forward.

"Around the corner; grab the horses," he panted. "The hellions had a bunch in there. We've got to get away before they get untangled. *Rurales* about, too, and if they grab us for a killing we'll never get out of their lousy jail. Here we are! Fork, feller, fork!"

Grant swung into the saddle, scooping up the split reins. Crowley flipped his slip knot loose, whirled his snorting horse and pounded up the trail at a dead run, Grant following.

"Can't risk the bridge — it may be guarded," he shouted. "Come on, feller; sift sand. We've got to get in the clear. You hurt much?"

"Just a scratch — take care of it later," Grant answered. He knotted the reins, let them fall on Smoke's neck and guided the big moros with his knees as he reloaded. His left hand was sticky with blood, but he knew the flow was slackening, the bullet gash in his arm nothing serious. Behind them the darkened saloon still seethed and bubbled with horrendous sound.

The trail followed the bend of the river, and they rode due north with the tawny flood of the Rio Grande sweeping past on their right. Crowley glanced about and peered at the rushing water, evidently on the lookout for landmarks.

They rode at top speed for nearly two miles; then Crowley pulled up, Grant jostling to a halt beside him.

"Here it is," he said, turning his horse's nose to the water. "Right across, feller."

"Good Lord, man! We can't swim that!" Grant protested. "The river's at flood."

"We'll make it," Crowley assured him. "Your horse will know what to do."

He urged his mount into the water as he spoke. Grant followed apprehensively. He heard Smoke's irons grate on stone; then the water was seething about the protesting animal's legs.

"Let him pick his own way, but keep his head up and don't let him stumble," Crowley said. "If you go off this rock on the down-side, the eddies and rapids will pound you to pieces in no time. Just ride straight behind me and you'll be okay."

Grant had not been particularly perturbed during the fight in the saloon. The action had been too swift and hectic to allow him time to be frightened. But now he admitted to himself that he was just plain scared. On his right the water frothed and stormed. To his left it raved and pounded against the rock barrier that retarded its rushing flood. He knew well what would be his fate if Smoke slipped off the narrow ledge, particularly on the down-stream side. He would be smashed to a pulp in that seething caldron of whirlpools and eddies. He set his jaw grimly and kept a tight hold on the reins as the shivering horse forged ahead in the wake of Crowley's big sorrel.

"Does the ledge go all the way across?" he called above the roar of the water.

"That's right," Crowley shouted back. "This is the old Indian Crossing. It's a ledge of limestone rock layin' just below the surface of the water. The Indians knew it long before the white men found it — been using it for years to slide wide-looped cows and horses across the river. In dry times the rock shows above the water. It was showing when I hit this section, and I gave it the once-over and made sure just where it started. Figured I might need it sometime if I took a notion to hustle across the river in a hurry. Guess I figured right. Didn't expect to try it with the water this high, though. This is a long ways from being a joke."

Grant thought so, too, as the water swirled higher and higher about Smoke's legs. He fervently hoped Crowley hadn't over-estimated the crossing's possibilities.

They were about halfway across when a rifle banged on the south bank. A slug whined overhead.

Crowley swore. "Somebody caught on! Ride, feller, ride!"

Another shot, and the passing slug fanned Grant's face with its lethal breath. He twisted in the saddle, stared back at the bank they had left. In the east, clouds hid the moon, but overhead, the stars were brilliant in a clear sky, and by their light he could see shadowy movement at the water's edge. He wished his big Winchester was snugged in the saddle boot beneath his left thigh, but contemplating a peaceful ride to town, he had left the long gun at the ranch-house. He estimated the distance. It was long range for a six-gun, but maybe he could throw a scare into the devils. He drew the big Colt, tipped the muzzle up and let drive till the six was empty.

A yell of pain, thin above the rushing water, was followed by a torrent of profanity.

"Good!" Shouted Crowley. "You winged one. Them ain't no *rurales* — that cussin' was in good United States. Come on; keep going before they get organized again."

Once again the unseen rifle blazed; but now they were more than two thirds across and didn't even hear the slug. Grant holstered his empty gun and gave all his attention to riding.

Several times before they reached the far bank, Jim Grant was sure the day of his death by drowning was at hand. Both horses were blowing hard and almost frantic with terror when they at long last sloshed through the shallows to safety.

"Street down there," said Crowley, gesturing to a sprinkling of lights a little way to the south. "Called Bruni Street, or some such loco name, I believe. Come on; we'll stop under one of those lights and have a look at your arm. I got salve and a roll of bandage in my pouch. Always pack 'em along with me; they've come in handy more than once."

The light in question was but a big lantern hung on a pole, but its glow was sufficient to reveal the ugly gash in the flesh of Grant's upper arm when he rolled up his sleeve.

"Nothing to it," said Crowley as he went to work with expert fingers. "Be sore tomorrow, but it'll soon heal up. You're lucky, feller; that was an out-and-out try at a snake-blooded killing if I ever saw one. Those hombres came in looking for you, and they had some of their pals stationed inside to take a hand if need be. Guess they didn't get time to horn in till it was too late. You did a swell job of gunslinging on the hellions."

"But the last one would have gotten me if it hadn't been for you," Grant replied. "He was lined on me dead centre, and my guns were empty when you threw down on him."

Crowley chuckled delightedly. "Guess he will have trouble breathing, wherever he is, with that hole in his neck," he chortled. "Did you see the blood squirt? Looked like somebody had cut loose with a fire hose. And the one you got in the face, he was a mess. Must have turned his head just as you pulled trigger, and the slug caught him sideways. Looked like raw steak the cook had been pounding with a cleaver. Told you they'd likely be after you, feller, after what you did to them up in the hills. Well, I've a notion they'll sort of walk around you from now on. It was some shindig, all right. Ain't had so much fun for a long time. There, that had ought to hold you. Let's go get a drink. I need one."

Over glasses in a quiet place on Juarez Avenue, they rehashed recent events.

"I believe you mentioned a hankering to tie onto a job of riding," Grant commented. "If so, reckon you'd better ride out to the spread with me tomorrow. I'm range boss, and I'll sign you on, if it's okay with you."

"Feller, that will be just fine!" Crowley agreed enthusiastically. "Say, this is my lucky night! Had a swell time and tied onto a job, too. Yep, I was sure lucky to run into you."

"And I was lucky that you did," Grant replied with conviction.

Deciding that they'd had enough excitement for one night, they stabled their horses, secured accommodations for themselves and went to bed.

CHAPTER
ELEVEN

Grant slept late. In fact, it was Zeke Crowley pounding on the door that finally aroused him.

"Just wanted to make sure you're okay," said the Montana puncher when he was admitted. "Sometimes a feller gets hurt worse in that kind of a shindig than he knows. That arm ain't swelling up, is it?"

"Don't think so," said Grant, flexing the member in question. "Feels a mite stiff, but that's about all."

"It's a tidy, sizable arm," Crowley commented approvingly. "You're bigger'n you look. What say we go get something to eat? I'm starved."

"That's a notion," agreed Grant, starting to dress. "Then we'll head for the spread, if it's all right with you."

"Don't ask nothing better," said Crowley. "I'm a mite tired of chuck line riding; hanker to eat regular for a spell and see a cow screw-tailing away from my loop. Loafing's all right for a while, but a feller who's always been used to working gets sort of fed up after a bit."

They ate and then put the rigs on their horses and set out for the Swinging J ranchhouse. Crowley nodded his approval as they rode across the gently rolling rangeland of the valley.

64

"Good pasture," he said, "mighty good pasture. But there's one thing I'd keep in mind, if I was you."

"What's that?" asked Grant.

"Fire," replied Crowley. "The grass is nigh belly-high on the horses, and after a while it'll be mighty dry. Wind blows up from the south-east most of the time, and sometimes blows hard. Let a grass fire get going good on range like this and you're in trouble. Tell you what I'd do, if I was you. I'd buy me some ploughs and have 'em handy. With a few good ploughs you can run furrows mighty fast and hold a fire back. Learned that trick up in the Panhandle, where the land is flat as a board and the needle and wheat grasses grow mighty tall. More'n one outfit has saved their buildings and most of their cows with that trick."

Grant nodded thoughtfully. "I've a notion you've got something there," he agreed. "Glad you mentioned it; I'll keep it in mind. We didn't have to worry much about grass fires in the Nueces country or around the Brazos, where I did most of my riding, but I know they are bad in other sections. Yes, I'll keep it in mind."

When they arrived at the ranch house, now practically completed, old Joel greeted Crowley cordially, and when informed of the part he had played in the Nuevo Laredo row, he shook the big puncher's hand with warmth.

"I'm mighty beholden to you, son," he told Crowley. "Would have felt mighty bad if something had happened to Jim."

A little later, Zeke Crowley looked about him with complacent satisfaction.

"You know, feller," he said to Grant, "I've a notion I've found myself a home."

"Hope so," Grant replied. "I think you'll be better off than mavericking around all over the map." Crowley nodded agreement.

Grant did keep in mind what Crowley said about grass fires, and it was the reason for his ride toward the northwest hills two days later.

The miles flowed past steadily under the big moros' irons, and as they neared the hills the country began to change. Groves and thickets became more numerous, with slopes and low hill crests. Finally, from one of the crests, Grant sighted the gleam of Camera Sanchez' wire, the posts that supported the taut strands marching steadily north like soldiers in single file. He rode down the long slope and reached the level ground below. After riding a quarter of a mile across the level ground, he entered a straggle of fairly dense thicket, Smoke picking his way through the bushes and avoiding as many thorns as possible. He poked his nose through a final fringe, and Grant saw the fence was less than a hundred yards distant.

He saw something else, something that instantly held his attention. Near the fence stood a saddled and bridled horse. On the ground lay strands of wire, and a slender figure in overalls, rough woollen shirt and a wide hat, was struggling with the top strand, apparently trying to join the severed ends and not having much luck at it.

Smoke paced slowly forward, his irons practically soundless on the thick grass. A dozen yards distant, Grant halted him and unforked. He decided the fence mender was just a kid, and not a very big one at that. No wonder he was having trouble with the heavy barbed strand. He was not surprised when a musical voice in the treble register made several pungent remarks apropos of the stubborn wire. Grant sauntered forward until he was within arm's length of the absorbed figure.

"Having trouble?" he asked.

Jim was totally unprepared for what happened next. The figure whirled around, and Grant looked down into the biggest and bluest eyes he had ever seen. A slender sun-golden hand flickered, and a gun muzzle was jammed against his ribs.

"Who the devil are you, and where'd you come from?" demanded the owner of the eyes and the gun.

Grant instantly decided it was no time for heroics; that gun prodding his middle was at full cock. But there was a gleam of amusement in his eyes as they rested on the small belligerent figure.

"Ma'am," he said, "if you'll just pen that hog-leg, I'll begin at the cradle and work all the way up."

The girl stared at him; then she flushed a little. She stepped back, uncocked the gun and leathered it.

"Sorry," she said. "Guess I made a mistake. I thought you were one of the hellions who cut this wire, coming back to stop me from mending it."

"Nope, I didn't cut it," Grant replied.

She continued to gaze at him. "Say, I know you!" she exclaimed. "You must be the Mr. Jim Grant who gave Cale Whitmer a thrashing. Glad you did it — Cale has needed taking down a peg for quite a while. Uncle Cam told me all about it. Understand you fought Cale over his beautiful cousin. Another conquest for the ravishing Norma, I suppose. Well, I don't blame you. She *is* beautiful, and smart. And I admire her for standing up to Cale and walking out on him like she did."

Grant merely said, "Yes, I'm Grant. And you?"

"I'm Lila McCarthy, the poor relation of the Sanchez family," she answered. "Uncle Cam took me in when Dad died, a couple of years back."

"And he makes you mend fence to pay for your keep?" Grant asked gravely.

"Nope," she replied. "He'll raise ned if he finds out. He's a Texas cowman if there ever was one, but he holds by the family tradition that a Sanchez woman must only be ornamental. I'm not ornamental, and I like ranch work."

Looking at her, Grant was inclined to disagree emphatically with the first half of the statement. She was small, but her figure was well nigh perfect, he thought. Not even the baggy overalls and the rough woollen shirt could conceal its graceful and alluring contours.

"It is heavy work for a girl, though," he said. "That's number nine twist and pulled tight. Let me have those pliers."

"Oh, I can handle it, I think," she protested. Nevertheless she surrendered the pliers. Grant turned to the fence.

The heavy wire hummed as he drew it taut. A couple of deft twists with the pliers, and the top strand was securely joined in such a manner that the break was almost imperceptible. He began to work on the second strand.

The girl watched him, a peculiar expression in her big eyes. Abruptly, with a petulant gesture, she swept the wide hat from her head and shook her wealth of glossy brown curls free.

Grant straightened up from joining the lowest strand, turned and for the first time got a really good look at her face.

It was a sweet face, wild and shy, the freckles powdering the bridge of her pert little nose and the dimple that came and went at one corner of her red mouth lending a touch of innocent diablerie. There was something elfin about her.

An inquiring snort from Smoke broke the spell. Grant chuckled under his breath and handed her the pliers.

"How come the wire was cut?" he asked casually.

She shrugged daintily. "To let the cows drift through. A lot of young and unbranded stuff on this north pasture. Plenty of them would have ambled out during the night, and in the morning they wouldn't have been anywhere around. The hellions must have kept tabs on the fence patrol, watched them head south for the ranch house and then gone to work."

Grant's eyes were abruptly grave. He scanned the slopes of the nearby hills, darkling and ominous as the sun sank behind the western crags.

"Didn't it occur to you that you might be incurring considerable personal danger by mending that fence, if whoever cut it happened to be keeping an eye on it?" he asked.

The big eyes widened and she looked a bit startled. "Why — I never thought of it," she confessed.

Grant nodded and continued to scan the slopes. "I think it would be a good notion for you to amble back to the ranch house," he said.

"You'll ride with me?"

Grant shook his head. "I think I'll ride around up here a bit," he parried. "Want to get a look at the canyons opening onto our range."

Lila McCarthy studied him a moment.

"You're not very good at lying, Mr. Grant," she observed.

"Now what the devil do you mean by that?" he demanded, looking a bit startled in turn.

"I mean that what you really plan to do is hang around here and see if anybody comes to find out how many cows drifted through that cut," she said. "Not a bad idea, at that. Might get a chance to plug one of the devils. We'll do just that."

Grant stared at her. "Miss McCarthy, you'll do no such thing!" He exploded. "You're going home."

"Nope, not unless you ride with me."

"All right," he said resignedly, "I'll ride with you."

But this exasperating small person had another surprise in store for him.

"You can ride if you wish," she said, "but you've given me a notion. I'm going to stay here and see if somebody does show up."

Jim Grant shook both fists in the air. Then abruptly he subsided to his normal cool and calculating self.

"Very well," he said with deceptive calmness. "We stay. But I'm telling you one thing, and I mean it. You'll do exactly as I tell you. I'd hate to manhandle a lady, but if you don't obey me, for your own protection I'll keep you quiet with a good solid punch to the jaw."

"I'll do just as you say, Jim, I promise," she answered meekly, adding irrelevantly, "I understand Cale Whitmer was quiet for quite some time after a good solid punch to the jaw. What do we do now?"

"Now," Grant replied, "we're forking our broncs and riding south."

CHAPTER
TWELVE

Grant and the girl rode steadily at a moderate pace. The riot of colours above dulled and tarnished until the whole vast sweep of the heavens was a steely grey. Misty stars began to appear, one by one, until the sky was sown with a myriad of softly glowing sparks. A whippoor-will called its plaintive note. An owl floated past on soundless wings. Wheeling bats uttered their sharp, needlelike cries. Then a vast silence settled over the rangeland, through which the soft thud of the horses' irons on the thick grass loudened. Lila glanced questioningly at Grant.

"Not yet," he told her.

Not until full dark had fallen did he alter their direction from south to an eastern course that finally pointed the horses' noses due north.

"I want to come in behind that thicket near the cut in the wire," he explained to his companion. "If anybody was watching from the hills, I think we fooled them. If they aim to investigate what was done to the cut wire, they'll soon be drifting down that way. From the thicket we'll have the advantage. Perhaps, if there are only two or three, we can drop a loop on one of the devils and persuade him to do a little talking. It appears organized rustling is going on in this section, and if we can learn who's back of it, there'll be a chance to bust it up."

"I see," she said. "I was wondering just what you had in mind, but I promised to do what you said and didn't ask any questions."

"You've been behaving very nicely, so far," he conceded.

"Thank you, sir," she murmured demurely.

Soon he knew the thicket must be close, and abruptly Smoke pricked his ears forward and blew softly through his nose.

Grant instantly pulled up, the girl halting beside him.

"What's the matter?" she whispered.

"I don't know," Grant whispered back, "but my horse says there's something ahead. May be only a coyote or a lion sneaked down from the hills, but it could be something else. Keep perfectly quiet and listen."

For long moments they sat motionless and listened, holding the reins taut lest the bit irons jingle, and heard nothing. But still Smoke peered with ears pricked forward and from time to time blew softly with flaring nostrils, a warning Jim Grant had long ago learned not to disregard.

"I'm afraid there's something more than a coyote or a cat in that chaparral," he whispered to the girl.

"But what does it mean?" she breathed.

"It means, if somebody *is* holed up in that brush heap, that we've been outsmarted. They were keeping tabs on us from up in the hills and figured we'd come back to see if the fence was cut again. With us out by the fence and them in the thicket, the advantage would be all on their side. Maybe I'm wrong, but I don't believe I am. Anyhow, I'm going to find out. Keep your reins taut, and if your horse acts like he's going to neigh, grab his nose. You don't have to worry about Smoke — he'll be quiet."

He dismounted lithely as he spoke.

"Let me go with you," she begged.

"No," he answered decisively. "One has a better chance of not getting spotted than two. You do as I tell you and stay here. You promised, remember."

"I wish I hadn't!" She breathed. "Be careful — Jim."

"I will — Lila," he replied, and glided away into the darkness.

Overhead, the cloud veil was thinning, and in the east was a bright spot. The moon had risen and was threatening to break through the shifting wrack.

It was nerve-wracking, creeping slowly along with that threatening spot in the east growing brighter and brighter; but he dared not increase his pace, especially as he drew nearer the thicket that was now taking form as a solid shape amid the shadows.

Grant reached the deeper gloom that shrouded the outer fringe of the growth and breathed a little easier. Now at least he would be on an even footing with the presumed rustlers, not a sitting quail out in the moonlight. He paused a long minute to peer and listen.

Overhead the leaves and interlacing branches were thinning, patches of sky showing through; Grant knew he must be nearing the outer fringe of growth and that the fence was but a few yards beyond. He slowed his pace still more, pausing often to peer and listen, but saw and heard nothing. He relaxed a bit but remained vigilant as he wormed along at a pace any able-bodied snail would have exceeded. Then abruptly he froze. Above him was a space of open sky with a star or two peering down inquiringly. But from the shadows in front came a sound that set his pulses to pounding — the sound of low voices.

The moon broke through the clouds, revealing four men grouped at the edge of the growth. It also revealed Jim Grant standing in an open space, like an actor spotlighted on a darkened stage.

There was a startled exclamation. Grant leaped sideways with all his strength and hurled himself down. A gun blazed and a bullet whipped through the leaves. Prone on the ground, Grant drew from his right hip and fired at the flash. There was a queer gurgling grunt, then a soft thud. Yells of anger arose, and a volley of shots. Grant rolled over and over, fired twice and rolled again. Answering slugs spattered the ground. One grazed his forehead, sending blood streaming into his eyes, half stunning him. He scrambled to his feet, ducked and weaved and fired three swift shots. Slamming the empty six into his sheath, he drew his other gun, crouched low and waited.

A voice rang out, "There's only one man in there! Fan out and get him!"

The brush crackled, and shots began coming from several directions. Jim knew he was in a bad spot. Another minute and he would be caught in a deadly crossfire. He held his own fire, peering to catch a glimpse of movement amid the shadows. The growth rustled as the outlaws moved to surround him, but they kept undercover and he was unable to line sights on one of the hellions.

From the far edge of the thicket came a tremendous crashing, two charging horses sounding like a dozen, and a volley of piercing yells. A gun cracked, and another. Grant knew the bullets were passing high overhead, but the outlaws didn't. With yells and curses they fled wildly, Grant speeding them on their way with a hail of lead. Hoofs thudded northward.

"Hold it, Lila, hold it!" Grant shouted.

Lila's sorrel loomed gigantic in the moonlight, Smoke beside him, and came to a halt beside Grant.

"Jim!" She cried. "Are you all right? Your face is covered with blood!"

"Just a scratch," he told her. He started to swing onto Smoke's back, then changed his mind. If he rode in pursuit of the fleeing rustlers, she would follow him, and she'd been exposed to enough danger for one night.

She was on the ground beside him, wiping the blood from his face with a small handkerchief; Grant assisted with a large one.

"This blasted section!" He growled. "I've been in it only a couple of weeks, and I've dodged more lead than during all the rest of my life. You all right?"

"Of course," she answered, "but are you? You're sure you're not hurt some place else?"

"I'm okay," he replied, and began reloading his guns. "But I wouldn't be if you hadn't happened along when

76

you did," he added. "They were closing in on me. I think I got one of the sidewinders. You stay put with the horses till I make sure."

He glided toward the edge of the growth, gun ready for instant action.

To his exasperation she didn't "stay put." She followed him. However, there was no need for apprehension; the crumpled form at the edge of the growth would take no more shots at anybody.

Grant stopped and turned the corpse over on its back. He gazed into a hardbitten face that was totally unfamiliar.

"Lila," he said, glancing over his shoulder, "I hate to ask you to do it, but I want you to take a good look at this devil on the chance that you might have seen him somewhere before."

The girl shuddered, but she obediently bent nearer the contorted face. She gazed at it for a long moment.

"Jim," she said slowly, "I believe I have seen him somewhere before, but where I haven't the slightest notion."

Grant nodded and straightened up. "Maybe some of the boys at your ranch may recognize him," he remarked. "We'll have to leave him where he is — can't risk tying him behind the saddle on one of our horses. We might need all they've got to give before we get home. Come on and let's get out of here. Those hellions might have others waiting for them up in the hills. We don't want to play our luck too strong."

He led the way back to the horses. Without further delay they mounted and rode south at a fast clip.

CHAPTER
THIRTEEN

Thoroughly worn out, Grant slept late. He was awakened by the sound of a piano and a voice singing, a pure, sweet contralto. He lay drowsily listening till the music stopped, then washed and dressed and descended the stairs, the treads of which were heavily carpeted.

He and Lila had a very enjoyable breakfast, and before they had finished, Camera Sanchez came in.

"The boys should be here 'most any time now with that body," he said. "I'm anxious to get a look at it."

Lila shuddered. "I don't want to see it again," she said. "It was awful."

Camera shrugged. "The hellion had it coming to him."

Shortly after they had finished eating and repaired to the living room, hoofs sounded outside. A moment later Jess Sanborn strode into the room. There was a peculiar expression on his lined face as he gazed at Grant.

"Sure that jigger you plugged wasn't just playing 'possum?" he asked without preamble.

"Well, if he was, he was doing it minus about half his neck," Grant replied. "The slug caught him in the throat and ploughed sideways."

"So I gathered from the looks of the grass at the edge of that thicket," Sanborn nodded. "Yep, we found bloodstains, but no body."

His hearers stared at him. "No body!" Grant repeated.

"That's right," said Sanborn. "Not a hair or hide of the skunk."

"But what does it mean?" asked Lila.

"I'd say it means that his pardners sneaked back after you were gone and packed it off," said Sanborn.

"But why?"

"I'd say because they were mighty anxious for nobody here to get a good look at him," Sanborn replied. "Yep, mighty anxious."

He stared out one of the big windows that faced to the west for a moment, then left the room. Camera Sanchez shook his head ruefully.

"Jess is set in his ways," he said. "He's convinced the hellion was one of Cale Whitmer's outfit. It does seem somebody was afraid he would be recognized."

"But not necessarily Whitmer or his hands," Grant pointed out. "He may have been associated with somebody in town, for instance; somebody who didn't want it known that one of his associates was mixed up in such an affair."

"Yes, that's possible," Sanchez admitted. "But who?"

"You know the section better than I do," Grant answered dryly.

"Yes, I guess I do," Sanchez said slowly. A sudden thought seemed to strike him; he started to speak, then apparently changed his mind.

"Yes, it could be somebody in town," he agreed. Grant was sure that was not what he had intended saying in the first place.

"Well, anyhow, thanks to you and Lila, we didn't lose any cows last night," he observed. "And we've been losing plenty in just that fashion. Not a great many at a time. A dozen head here, a score there, a hundred some place else. It's been going on for quite a while now."

Grant looked sober.

"And you haven't been able to catch them at it?" he asked.

"Not so far," Sanchez replied. "You and Lila are the only ones who have even managed to run into them. I have a lot of land. It's difficult to patrol it even in the daytime, let alone at night, and they're very clever."

Grant asked another question. "Where do they run the cows?"

"Eventually across the Rio Grande, I'd say," Sanchez replied. "Good market for wet beefs down there. Buyers very often resell them on this side of the Line in some other section."

"But how do they get them across the river?" Grant persisted.

"It would seem the logical way would be to run them east and through the hills that curve to the south," Sanchez replied a trifle hesitantly.

"Or west and across Cale Whitmer's holdings," said a voice from the window. Turning, they saw Jess Sanborn strolling away.

"We have trailed several bunches west," Sanchez was forced to admit. "But we always lost them. A veritable network of old trails through those hills, and the ground is very hard and stony."

Grant nodded, his eyes thoughtful. He had a theory of his own relative to the disposal of the wide-looped cows, but he didn't mention it to Camera; he wanted to try it out before mentioning it to anybody.

Camera Sanchez urged Grant to spend another night at the hacienda; but the latter declined the invitation.

"Uncle Joel will be getting worried about me," he explained to his host.

"Well, come again soon," Sanchez said.

Lila added, "And I promise next time I won't poke a gun in your ribs."

Joel Collison's reaction to Grant's story of what had happened the day before was wrathful and profane.

"Darned snake-blooded thieves!" He rumbled. "And Sanchez has been losing lots of cows. Suppose we'll be next."

Grant was of the same opinion and decided to anticipate the rustlers with some remedial precautions. Two days later he rode north by west into the hills.

Camera Sanchez hadn't exaggerated. The uplands were a maze of trails. And though low, little more than a steep rise from the valley floor, they were extremely rugged.

For a couple of miles he followed a trail with quickened interest, but the ground was growing very stony and other trails joined or crossed the one he was following. Soon he was hopelessly confused. He pulled up at a forks, rolled a cigarette and smoked thoughtfully.

"Smoke," he told the moros, "we're getting nowhere fast. Trying to follow anything through this mess of snake tracks is just a waste of time. We're going to try another angle; to reach the river those cows had to cross the range-land, and at the base of this mess of rocks the grass is sparse."

With considerable difficulty he made his way to the level ground below the hills. Here he first back-tracked for nearly three miles, and found nothing. Turning Smoke, he rode west again at a fast pace until he reached the place where he had descended from the hills. He slowed the moros, scanning the ground with eyes that missed nothing, and that saw nothing to indicate cows had recently passed that way.

He rode on until he spotted a shallow gorge from which flowed a small stream. He turned into the gulch and soon found thickets that promised a plenitude of dry wood. Getting the rig off Smoke and turning him loose to graze, he kindled a fire and went about preparing something to eat. Having expected to spend a night out, he had provided a store of staple provisions. From his saddle pouches he took a hunch of bread, coffee, bacon, and some eggs carefully wrapped against breakage. A little flat bucket and a small skillet were all the cooking utensils needed. Soon coffee was bubbling in the bucket, bacon crisping in the skillet. He fried three eggs in the bacon grease until they were well blackened on both sides and of a consistency guaranteed to give a rhinoceros indigestion. Then he ate his simple meal with relish, smoked a couple of cigarettes, and, after cleaning up, spread the blanket he had carried rolled behind the cantle and very quickly was sound asleep.

CHAPTER
FOURTEEN

Dawn found him awake. After cooking some breakfast, he rode out of the gorge and continued west. Mile after mile he rode, and found no evidence of the passage of cattle headed toward the Rio Grande. Finally the hills petered out and the rangeland stretched unbroken north and west and south. Rounding the tip of the hills, he rode north for a number of miles. When the sun was slanting westward, he pulled to a halt with a disgusted grunt.

"Smoke," he said, "no cows came west through those darned bumps on the ground. They didn't turn south anywhere, either. We've been following a cold trail, but it's given me a notion. They *did* head west after being rustled from Camera Sanchez' range, if that's where they came from. No matter where they came from, they were driven west for a way not long ago. Yes, horse, I'm beginning to have a notion. Let's go home!"

It was a long ride back to the Swinging J ranch house, and midnight had come and gone before Grant stabled his weary horse. Late as it was, however, a light burned in the ranch house living room, and old Joel Collison sat under the lamp smoking.

"Figured you'd get in some time tonight," he replied when Grant expressed surprise that he should still be up at such an ungodly hour. "Figured you'd want to know what happened." He paused to tamp down the tobacco in his pipe bowl.

"What did happen?" Grant asked.

"We lost our first bunch of cows," Collison said. "Nigh onto a hundred head of prime beef critters."

"Sure they didn't stray some place?"

"Nope, they didn't stray," Collison answered. "It was a bunch fattening over on the east pasture. We trailed them for a piece."

"To the river?"

"Nope, they didn't head for the river; they headed into the hills and went west. We trailed them west for quite a way and then lost them among those rocks and tracks up there, just like Sanchez says he always lost bunches he followed. Jim, I'm beginning to wonder about that Whitmer feller."

Grant was silent for a moment; he didn't know just what to think about Cale Whitmer. He rolled a cigarette and lighted it and then spoke.

"Uncle Joel," he said, "yesterday — day before yesterday now — I followed a bunch of cows west through the hills and lost the trail. I didn't try to pick it up again, at least not for long. I rode down to the prairie and along the base of the hills until they petered out; then I rode north for quite a way. And nowhere did I see any signs of cows coming down from the hills. And if they had come down, they couldn't have avoided leaving signs of their passage on the soft ground where the grass is sparse at the base of the ridge. If they went west they stayed in the hills."

"Figure they went north?"

"They *could* have gone north," Grant conceded, "but if they did, where the devil were they headed for? Fact is, I don't know where they went, but I intend to find out."

"I hope so," said Collison. "A hundred head at a clip is too much. Let that keep up and we'll be out of business before we know it. And the same goes for Sanchez. Fact is, he's worse off than I am — he owes money to the bank. Had to borrow some to finish paying for all that wire he strung."

"With his holding as security," Grant commented.

"Of course," nodded Collison. "You can't borrow much on cattle nowadays; banks don't like to take the risk. Of course the spread is worth more than he borrowed on it, including some additional he borrowed a year or so ago to tie him over when the going was bad. But he has to scratch to meet his payments and the face of the note when the balance falls due, or so he gave me to understand. He can't afford to lose a lot of cows, either. Well, let's go to bed; maybe we can figure something tomorrow."

Jim Grant evolved a carefully thought out plan by which he hoped to deal the rustlers a telling blow; but with Scotch reticence, he neglected to take others into his confidence before he was ready to put the plan into action. And from this oversight came trouble.

For impulsive, belligerent Zeke Crowley had worked out a little plan of his own.

86

So the evening after Grant returned from his fruitless exploration of the northern hills, Zeke Crowley and eight picked men rode east by slightly south through the twilight.

What Crowley failed to realize was that the crests of the hills curving toward the south provided an excellent watch-tower for anybody interested in observing activities on the Swinging J rangeland below.

"As I said, I figure the hellions will be coming back tonight or tomorrow night to knock off another bunch," Crowley told his companions. "Now I've been riding quite a bit over to the east for the past few days. I figure there's just one place where cows can go up those slopes; every place else is too steep and rocky. So if there's only one way for them to go up, that's the way they'll have to go up. I figure the devils will make a try for a bunch around midnight or maybe a little later — that's the way that sort usually operates. We'll ride up the slope to the top and hole up and wait for 'em. We'll be all set to blow 'em from under their hats."

"Going to hit 'em as they head down to the pasture?" A young cowboy asked.

"Nope, we'll let 'em go ahead and round up the cows," Crowley replied. "Coming back, they'll be bunched behind the herd and not expecting anything to happen. Apt to be looking sharp as they go down, but once they tie onto the beefs and start back, they won't be worried about anything."

The others nodded approval.

Long before the "posse" reached the hills, full dark had fallen. The sky was brilliant with stars, and by their light and that of a low moon in the east, objects were visible for a long distance across the prairie. The night was very still, but as they drew near the base of the slopes, somewhere up in the rocky, brush-grown heights an owl hooted three times. In the distance a coyote yipped. After that the silence remained unbroken.

Crowley and his men began climbing what appeared to have once been a trail. It zigzagged up the slope so that nowhere was the going excessively steep.

"Cows could make it up here, all right," remarked one of the hands. "I've a notion you've got the right of it, Zeke. Hope the thieves show up tonight; I'm itching for a whack at 'em."

"Better stop talking from now on," Crowley advised. "Sounds carry a long way on a night like this. I wish the horses' irons didn't make so much of a clatter, but it's early, and it ain't likely anybody will be along for quite a while yet."

After better than a half-hour of slow riding they reached the crest of the slope, where the ground levelled off for a short distance ahead and was thickly brush-grown. And as they topped the hill, standing out hard and clear in the moonlight, they were met by a blast of gunfire, the reports ringing out like thunder in the vast stillness.

Three saddles were emptied by that first murderous volley. The remaining cowboys jerked their Colts and fired in the direction of the shooting, for there was nothing to see. Again the hidden guns boomed. A fourth man fell to lie motionless.

"Back!" bellowed Crowley. "Back! It's a trap."

The four hands still able to ride whirled their horses and fled back down the slope. Zeke Crowley, wounded in three places, lingered long enough to haul his Winchester from the saddle boot and empty the magazine into the brush, swinging the muzzle back and forth. A yell echoed the reports, and a wailing curse. Crowley wheeled his mount and rode at breakneck speed after his companions.

"Got one of 'em, maybe two," he muttered thickly, reeling and rocking in the saddle, gripping the horn for support.

At the bottom of the slope he overtook the others, who had pulled up to wait for him.

"Ride!" He gasped. "Ride fast! If they follow us down we'll be settin' quail out on the prairie — it's bright as day."

"You hurt much, Zeke?" One called as they got under way.

"Chunk of meat knocked off my ribs, another out of my leg, and I think I got a hole through my left arm," Crowley mumbled. "I'll make out. Anybody else get it?"

One cowboy had a bullet-gashed cheek, another a slight shoulder wound. Crowley soon decided that his own injuries, while painful, were comparatively slight. He had lost a good deal of blood, but he knew the flow was slackening. He set his teeth against the pain and rode on grimly.

CHAPTER
FIFTEEN

When Grant and Collison reached Laredo, they stabled their horses and then repaired to Potter's General Store, where old Joel made the final payment on his newly constructed ranchhouse and other buildings.

Frank Potter was highly pleased at the successful consummation of the project and said so.

"Better than I'd hoped for at first," he declared. "I was expecting trouble of some sort every day. Mighty glad nothing happened, and it's beginning to look like nothing will. Cale Whitmer seems to have cooled down a lot. Hasn't been making any threats of late about running everybody out of the section, like he used to do. Maybe the walloping Jim gave him took some of the fire out of him."

He paused, and his hearers waited expectantly, for they sensed that the storekeeper had something more to say.

"Fact is, I can't quite understand Cale's change in attitude," he added. "It's funny. I don't figure he'd give up a fight so easy. Yes, something funny about it, and I can't help but feel he's got something up his sleeve. My advice would be to keep an eye on him."

"Oh, I reckon he's got sense enough to know when he's licked," old Joel observed. "Guess he decided if he tackled Sanchez and us both, he might be biting off a mite more than he could chaw."

"Maybe," acceded Potter. Jim Grant thought he didn't sound convinced. In fact, Grant was not himself wholly in agreement with Collison's optimistic surmise. He had an uneasy premonition that they were not yet finished with Cale Whitmer.

Collison and the storekeeper began going over a list of supplies needed at the ranch house. Potter promised to fill the order and deliver it without delay. They left the store. Outside, old Joel chuckled a bit ruefully.

"What I handed Potter just about cleaned me of ready cash," he confessed. "Jim, we've got to get a shipping herd together. I figure we can comb out enough good stuff to round one out. The critters have been putting on weight fast. Let's go to the telegraph office, and I'll get in touch with a buyer I know how to reach and have had dealings with before."

At the telegraph office, Collison sent a wire that was answered within an hour.

"He'll handle 'em," he said, passing the message to Grant. "Will come over from Corpus Cristi as soon as I give the word we're ready. Reckon next we'd better arrange with the railroad folks for cars. How long do you figure it'll take to get a herd ready to roll?"

Grant made a few mental calculations and announced the result.

"Fine!" said Collison. "Let's see the railroad people right away."

Twilight was deepening before all the chores were finished, and both felt the need of something to eat.

"That Montezuma place is as good as any, I reckon," said Collison. "Might get to see that purty gal you had the fight with Whitmer over, too."

Grant didn't argue, and they headed for the saloon. They located a table and sat down.

"There she is," chuckled Collison, "over by the orchestra. Reckon you'd better ask her for a dance, Jim."

"I'm going to eat," Grant replied shortly.

"I'm in favour of it," said Collison, "but at your age a gal should come first."

"Not when I'm hungry," Grant declared. Collison chuckled again and did not press the point.

However, Grant was not so indifferent as he pretended to be. His glance kept straying to the far edge of the dance floor where Norma stood talking with the orchestra leader. He wondered if she would speak to him. She could hardly have missed seeing them enter and cross the room, but to all appearances she was oblivious to his presence.

He happened to catch old Joel's twinkling eye fixed on him and resolutely turned his attention to his food. He looked up as the rancher uttered an exclamation.

"Here comes Camera Sanchez!" Collison ejaculated. "And blazes! Look what he's got with him! Is *she* an eyeful!"

Grant was willing to concede that Lila McCarthy *was* an eyeful. Others were evidently of the same opinion, for there was a universal turning of heads as she crossed to the table. But the amusement in her blue eyes did not add to his peace of mind. He wondered if her impish sense of humour had deliberately planned this meeting, although it was hardly likely that she could have known that he had picked this particular day to come to town. He also felt that Camera Sanchez was not as comfortable as he might have been, although his manner was casual as he introduced old Joel to Lila.

As the orchestra began a dreamy Mexican waltz, Grant resolved to do something to relieve the tension.

"Care to dance?" He asked Lila.

"I'd love to," she replied.

Afterwards, Grant started to lead her back to the table, but Lila stopped him.

"I think you should ask Norma to dance," she said.

"She'd very probably refuse," he answered.

"Oh, no, she won't," Lila stated. "Go ask her — the music's starting again."

Grant hesitated, but the laughter in her eyes decided him. He strode across to where the red-haired girl was standing.

"May I have this one?" he asked.

"If you wish," she replied. "As I told you once before, that's what I'm here for."

Grant set his teeth and did not reply. He encircled her waist and they glided out onto the floor.

"Cale was here to see me this afternoon," she said suddenly.

"Make more trouble?"

Norma shook her head. "No, he seems to have cooled down a good deal. He asked me to have a drink with him, and we sat and talked. Seems strange, but he doesn't appear to hold any grudge against you. He said it was a fair fight and you won it fairly. Then he made a rather puzzling remark. He said he was sort of sorry that you would get caught in the squeeze. I asked him what he meant, but he just smiled and started talking of something else."

"I wonder what he did mean," Grant remarked thoughtfully.

"Hard to tell, but he definitely has something in mind," she answered. "I'm glad to see you are on good terms with Lila McCarthy; she's a nice girl. But don't get that mixture of Irish and Spanish blood riled up."

The music ceased and they stepped apart. "Won't you come over and have a glass of wine with us?" Grant invited.

"No," she said shortly, and left him. Grant shrugged and walked back to the table, where Lila greeted him with a gay smile. He did not see Norma Whitmer glance over her shoulder, her eyes suddenly wistful.

Shortly afterward, Lila and Sanchez departed. "A few chores to do and then back to the spread," Camera explained. "Want to be up early in the morning. Come and see us soon, both of you."

"Yes, please do," Lila chimed in.

Old Joel's eyes followed her to the door and then glanced toward the dance floor.

"By gosh, I don't know which is the purtier of the two!" He said. "Now, Jim, if this was just the Pacific Islands section, where a man can have as many wives as he wants, you'd be all hunky-dory."

94

"Oh, sure," Grant snorted. "One of them laughs at me and the other one snaps at me. I think I'll stay faithful to my horse; I can always figure just what he's going to do."

It was still dark when Grant was awakened by a hammering on his door. He opened it to admit Dolph Rader, one of the Swinging J hands.

"What the devil!" He exclaimed. "What brings you here, Dolph?"

Rader told him, explaining what had happened in the hills to the east. "I come for the doctor," he concluded, "and figured you ought to know about it. They told me at the Montezuma where you aimed to sleep."

Grant began getting into his clothes. "Go wake Uncle Joel, third door down the hall," he directed. "We'll be ready to ride pronto. You saw the doctor?"

"Yep," replied Rader. "Chances are he's already on his way. He was dressing when I left. Don't know as he's needed bad, but Crowley's purty well shot up and a couple more of the boys got punctures."

Grant nodded. He did not comment on Crowley's loco action. No sense in jumping on Zeke; he had acted for the best and had made a mistake, that was all. Grant was more inclined to blame himself for not having taken the others into his confidence; then the impulsive Crowley would not have gone sashaying off on his own. Well, that was water under the bridge and there was no use crying about it.

They overtook the doctor, an old frontier practitioner, about halfway from town and accommodated their speed to his. Upon reaching the ranch house, he patched up the wounded hands and allowed that Crowley, the most seriously injured, would be out looking for a chance to get hanged in a week or so.

Next came the grim chore of bringing in the bodies of the slain punchers. Grant approached the hills warily and had his men well spaced while ascending the slope.

They reached the crest without incident and found the four bodies where they had fallen; the horses, their rigs intact, were grazing on the sparse grass that clothed the hilltop.

"A smart bunch, all right," Grant commented. "Didn't touch anything that might tie them up with it."

Joel Collison swore bitterly as he gazed at the dead men, two of whom had worked for him for many years. The Swinging J hands said nothing, but vengeance was written indelibly on every face.

The bodies were roped to the saddles, and the dreary cavalcade began the return trip to the ranch house.

CHAPTER
SIXTEEN

During the ten days that followed, Jim Grant was too busy to do much meditating. There were plenty of cattle on the Swinging J range, but the majority still showed the effects of the long and hard drive from the Nueces. A great deal of careful combing was necessary to get together an acceptable shipping herd. Buyers were finicky and, in a tight market, were in a position to pick and choose. Joel Collison, however, enjoyed an excellent reputation with a big eastern buyer, which was an advantage.

"But we can't let him down," Collison said. "I've always given him the best, and that's what he'll expect."

"That's what he'll get," Grant replied. "We've got our work cut out for us, now that the cows are well scattered and are holing up to escape the heat, but there's plenty of good stuff available."

On the fourth day, Camera Sanchez visited the Swinging J. "Twice within the week my wire's been cut," he announced. "We're still checking to find out how many head we lost, but I'm afraid it's plenty."

"It's not an ordinary brush-popping outfit operating in this section," Grant declared. "They're organized, and they must have market contacts, presumably south of the Rio Grande, although possibly elsewhere."

"Beginning to look like it might be elsewhere," said Sanchez. "The river's really been in flood for the past week. No swimming cows across it, but just the same we've been losing cattle."

"They could have a holding spot somewhere in the hills or beyond," Grant observed thoughtfully.

"They could," Sanchez agreed. "Perhaps somewhere in the brush country. Be like trying to find a tick on a sheep's back, locating it in that tangle. I've complained to the sheriff, but he admits he's helpless. He has been riding the hills and the brush with a couple of deputies, and getting nowhere."

"Had no luck with those killers who did for our boys," remarked Collison. "He came out pronto when we notified him what happened, interviewed Zeke and the others and rode over to where it happened. Managed to follow the trail they left for a piece, then lost it, of course. They could have taken any of those snake tracks."

Sanchez nodded gloomy agreement. For years the section had been a paradise for rustlers. Sheriffs and Texas Rangers had run down a number of the thieves, but more invariably showed up sooner or later. But never before had there been such organized and steadily successful depredations.

"Somewhere a jigger with brains is sitting back and directing the moves," Grant said. "If we could just drop a loop on him, the rest would be easy."

"Uh-huh," nodded Sanchez, "but who is he and where is he?"

"I don't know who he is, but in my opinion he has his headquarters in Laredo," Grant said. "I expect a lot of folks will be greatly surprised when he's finally corralled."

"You don't figure that Whitmer gent is the hellion back of it all?" Old Joel asked curiously.

"I have no way of knowing whether or not Whitmer is mixed up in the business, but I don't think he has the brains to run such an organization," Grant replied. "If he is mixed up in it, I'd say he's being directed by somebody with a lot more savvy. I never met him but once, remember, but it was a rather personal meeting. My estimate of him is that he is the charging shorthorn type, governed largely by his emotions. A smart man playing on those emotions might be able to persuade him to enter into something against his own best judgment." He paused a moment, then continued:

"There is one angle worthy of consideration. So far as I have been able to learn, the spreads to the east and west have not lost any cows beyond the usual pilfering of brush poppers. The organized bunch is concentrating on the Rafter S and the Swinging J, as if they had an animus where the two outfits are concerned."

"Whitmer certainly has no use for me," Sanchez remarked.

"Exactly," Grant said. "So the logical conclusion is that he would get personal gratification from causing you as much trouble as possible. Oh, it's not hard to make out a case against Whitmer, but as I said before, I don't believe he's got the brains or ability to manipulate such an operation. If he's mixed up in it, and I'm not intimating that he is, there's a smarter man somewhere in the background pulling the wires. The question is, who?"

Camera Sanchez said nothing for several moments; then he appeared to make up his mind about something.

"Jim," he said, "perhaps you'll remember that one time I was here I mentioned that Whitmer had been seen associating with a man who runs a shady saloon down by the bridge, a fellow named Garland Shane; some folks call him Whispering Shane. He's a good deal of a character, is Shane. Has a share in several business enterprises and holds mortgages on a good deal of Laredo real estate. His interests are diversified, and, as a rule, lucrative. In addition to other holdings, he owns or partly owns several small steamboats that do a thriving trade with the Mexican villages between Rio Grande City and Brownsville. Sometimes they get up this far, but not often; depends on the state of the river. Has a finger in the political pie, too. Sort of a political boss of the section, and has connections over to the capital.

"There's never been anything proved against Shane, but he's believed to deal in smuggled goods and such things I don't say he's back of the wide-looping, but I consider him capable of just that. One of my Mexican tenant farmers who hangs out there some told me that several times Shane and Whitmer have gone into the back room together and closed the door. They seem to have a good deal to say to each other."

"Interesting," Grant commented. "I think I'll have a look at Mr. Shane."

"He's nothing to look at," said Sanchez. "A scrawny little shred of a man. Nothing remarkable about him except his eyes, which seem to brighten when he talks. Makes me think of lightning bugs. I can't conceive what Cale Whitmer would have in common with him. But whatever it is, you can wager it'll end to Shane's advantage, and Whitmer will be left holding the sack."

Grant digested this bit of information.

As it happened, that very night Jim Grant was being discussed by Whispering Shane and Lafe Haskins.

"Seems you didn't have any luck with him either," Haskins remarked.

"That's right," admitted Shane. "I thought we were all set to get rid of him over in Nuevo Laredo, but he killed two of the boys who were handed the chore of eliminating him, and that big cowhand he was hobnobbing with over there did for the other one, and they got away. Rode the Indian Crossing with the river at flood! They should have drowned."

"I told you he's a devil," growled Haskins. "The boys were sure they had a trap all set for him up by Sanchez' wire, but he slipped out of that one, too, and killed Russ Eaton to boot. Fortunately they had sense enough to sneak back and pack off Eaton's body. Wouldn't have been so good if Eaton had been brought in and folks remembered that he'd worked here in the saloon."

Shane nodded but did not otherwise comment.

"And over by the east hills," Haskins continued, "Grant had been spotted snooping around, and the boys were on the lookout for him. When they saw those Swinging J hellions riding that way after dark, they naturally assumed Grant was with them. He wasn't; that night he was here in town. The devil gets all the breaks."

"Lucky for the boys he wasn't with that bunch," Shane remarked. "They should have had sense enough to know he wasn't; Grant would never have ridden across the moonlit prairie that way. The chances are the first hint they'd have gotten that he was anywhere around would have been when he blew them from under their hats. We'll forget him for the time being; we've got other things to think about. Whitmer is all set to make his move as soon as I give the word. Yes, we'll forget Grant for a while, until I figure something else that may work. Blast him! I wish I could forget him altogether. He's the one angle that's got me worried."

"Don't see there's anything he can do about it, once Whitmer makes his move," said Haskins. "The affair will then be in the hands of the courts and the land office, and I don't think even Grant can drop a loop on them."

"Maybe not," Shane replied morosely, "but I wouldn't put it past him to pull something out of a hat. The hellion is shrewd. Okay, get busy with your chores. You seem to be doing all right so long as you don't tangle with Grant; I'm afraid he's too much for you and you'd better stay away from him. Next time he's liable to slice off more than a finger."

Haskins' face was black with rage at Shane's mockery, but he merely ground his teeth, scratched his newly grown beard viciously and swore under his breath.

The Swinging J herd rolled to Laredo at daybreak the following morning. Nearly all the Swinging J hands rode with it. It was highly unlikely that an attempt on the cows would be made on the open range, but Grant was taking no chances.

However, Laredo was reached without mishap. On a siding stood a string of stock cars waiting to receive their charges. The cows were run into the loading pens, shunted to the chutes and into the cars. The Swinging J punchers were old hands at the business and worked with efficiency and dispatch. Door after door banged shut on the bawling critters. In a surprisingly short time the chore was finished and the cowboys turned loose for a night on the town.

Jim Grant heaved a sigh of relief as the long train pulled out. Now the cows were the railroad's worry, not his. He and Collison headed for the Montezuma and something to eat.

Norma Whitmer was on the dance floor. She nodded to him but did not approach his table. Grant thought she looked tired and listless.

After they had finished eating, he and Collison sat and smoked for a while. Finally old Joel knocked out his pipe and glanced across the room.

"See the old jiggers we were playing cards with the other night are at it again," he observed. "I think I'll join them for a few hands. Want to come along?"

"I believe I'll take a walk," Grant declined. "Not much in the mood for poker right now."

Collison nodded and crossed to the card table, leaving Grant to his own devices.

Grant decided that this would be a good time to have a look at the saloon down by the bridge run by the gentleman Camera Sanchez called Whispering Shane. He left the Montezuma and made his way along Convent Avenue to the waterfront. On Zaragoza Street, between Flores and San Agustin Avenues, he found the saloon, a big place not too well lighted and with "Shane's" across the plate glass windows. He hesitated a moment, then pushed through the swinging doors.

The place was crowded, and his entrance attracted no attention. He found a place at the bar and ordered a drink. Glass in hand, he turned and surveyed the room. He was anxious to locate Whispering Shane and get a good look at him.

At first he had no success. There was nobody behind or at the bar who answered to Shane's description, or at the nearby tables. He contemplated a closed door that doubtless led to a rear room. Perhaps Shane was in there. Again he turned his attention to the room, and did locate Shane, easily recognizable from Camera Sanchez description.

He was seated at a corner table on the far side of the room, conversing with a big man with a heavy black beard who gestured as he talked.

Grant studied the saloonkeeper. He was ready to agree with Sanchez that Shane wasn't much to look at

— a very ordinary appearing individual, the kind one would pass on the street without a second glance.

Grant's gaze dropped to Shane's hands, which lay on the table top. They were large hands for so small a man, and powerful-looking. And, Grant noted, they were perfectly still. He studied Shane for several minutes, but not once did those capable-looking hands move.

He turned his attention to Shane's table companion and experienced a vague feeling that the fellow's face was familiar. Where had he seen that craggy brow and those deepset eyes before? He wracked his memory without results and was ready to give up when the man raised his right hand and gestured to drive home some point he was making. Grant's lips pursed in a soundless whistle.

That right hand was minus the index finger!

CHAPTER
SEVENTEEN

Grant finished his drink and walked out. He could always think better in the open air, and abruptly he had plenty to think about.

So Lafe Haskins *was* in Laredo, doubtless had been from the very first, his appearance greatly altered by the beard. And he was consorting with Whispering Shane! Grant digested this fact thoroughly, recalling that this wasn't the first time Lafe Haskins had visited Laredo.

But where did Cale Whitmer fit into the picture? Grant didn't know and wished he did.

Grant walked about aimlessly for some time, pondering what he had learned and coming to no definite conclusion. Finally he gave up in disgust and returned to the Montezuma.

He found old Joel sitting alone at a table, a full glass in front of him.

"Just couldn't seem to get interested in cards," he explained as he beckoned a waiter.

Norma Whitmer was on the floor, dancing with a fresh-faced young cowhand who gave every evidence of being badly smitten. She appeared to have thrown off her former depressed mood and was chatting gaily with her partner. Grant watched her for a few minutes, shrugged and turned to Collison. Old Joel eyed his drink meditatively and downed it at a swallow.

"Jim," he said, "I just can't seem to cotton to things in town tonight. What do you say we get out of here and head for home? It's a nice night for a ride."

"Suits me," Grant acceded. He cast a final glance toward the dance floor and followed Collison out.

Although Zeke Crowley was well on the way to recovery from his wounds, Grant had thought it unwise for him to take the ride to Laredo. So he and Gene Kelton and a couple more hands had been left behind when the drive set out. Kelton reported to the ranch house the following morning.

"I was right," he told Grant. "We're short nearly three hundred head on the north pasture."

Grant questioned Kelton closely and decided the old puncher knew what he was talking about. Something had to be done.

The upshot of the matter was that Jim Grant again rode into the hills. This time, however, he did not attempt to trail the stolen cows west. Despite what lanky Jess Sanborn and others of the Rafter S thought, Grant was convinced that the purloined stock did not cross Cale Whitmer's holding to reach the Rio Grande. He was playing a hunch that he hoped would pay off as he searched the hills to the north. Late in the afternoon, he discovered indubitable evidence that cattle had recently passed that way — headed east!

"Smoke, I was right," he told the big moros. "They run them west to throw off pursuit, lose the trail in that mess of tracks and rocks over there, then circle back east. And I'm willing to bet they veer them south to where the hills turn and approach the river. Yes, my hunch was a straight one. Horse, somebody is going to get a surprise."

Greatly elated, he rode home under the stars. He did not reveal to anyone what he had discovered, but the following evening he rode due south by east as if he were headed for Laredo.

Before he reached the town, however, he veered to his left and rode in a more easterly direction through the deepening shadows of the twilight. Not until he could see the dark loom of the spur of hills to the south did he draw rein. On his right was the Rio Grande, no great distance away. He considered the prospect for some minutes, then rode into a fairly dense thicket. He dismounted, flipped the bit from Smoke's mouth and turned him loose to graze on the sparse grass that grew between the chaparral trunks. Taking up a position at the edge of the growth, he made himself as comfortable as conditions permitted and settled down to watch. Nothing could pass down from the hills and approach the river and not be within the range of his vision.

Hour after hour he watched and waited, and saw nothing but the lonely stars and heard nothing other than the occasional call of some night bird and the soft whisper of the wind stirring the leaves over his head.

The great clock in the sky wheeled westward; the stars paled from gold to silver, dwindled to needle points of steel. In the east, a pearly glow deepened to tremulous pink. Grant mounted and rode home. He was not particularly disappointed over the negative results of his all night vigil. The rustlers certainly didn't knock off a herd every night.

The next night was a repetition of the first, and equally barren of results. The third night was also productive of nothing. Grant rode home at dawn in a very disgusted frame of mind. He experienced a disquieting foreboding that his hunch wasn't such a bright one, after all. Well, he'd try and find out about that. He slept till mid-afternoon then saddled up and headed for the Rafter S.

Camera Sanchez was pottering about outside the ranch-house when Grant arrived at the hacienda. He shouted a cordial greeting and summoned a wrangler to take care of Smoke.

"Come on in," he said. "About time for coffee and a snack." He had started to lead the way up the veranda steps when Grant stopped him.

"Just a minute," said the Swinging J range boss. "I want to ask a question. Did you lose any more cows lately?"

"Yep," Camera replied in rueful tones. "Night before last the north wire was cut and maybe a hundred head drifted through. The hellions appear to be hep to every move the patrols make and are always one jump ahead of us."

"Sure about it?" Grant persisted.

"Of course I'm sure," Sanchez replied, a note of irritation creeping into his voice. "What you getting at, Jim?"

"Let's go inside and I'll tell you," Grant answered.

When they entered the living room, Grant glanced around expectantly. However, Lila McCarthy was not present; he experienced a slight twinge of disappointment. After all, she was good company.

Camera Sanchez gave some orders to the cook and turned to Grant.

"Now, what you got to tell me?" he asked.

Grant began at the beginning, citing his reasons for believing the stolen cattle did not pass across Cale Whitmer's holdings and why he did believe that they circled back east to reach the Rio Grande by way of the southerly spur of the hills. Sanchez sat silent in absorbed attention.

"But the bunch you say you lost the other night certainly did not pass that way," Grant concluded.

"And what's the answer?" Sanchez asked.

"Beginning to look like there might be something to your guess that there could possibly be a holding spot somewhere to the north. It doesn't seem reasonable, but where the devil do they go?"

Sanchez shook his head. "It's beyond me," he admitted. "But I'm sort of glad it appears they don't go across Whitmer's holdings. I haven't much use for Cale, but old Silas Whitmer and my Dad were mighty close friends. I'd hate to think Silas Whitmer's son was mixed up in something like that. Having a row with me over a difference of opinion is one thing, but thieving and murder is something else."

Grant nodded but did not speak, for Sanchez still looked contemplative.

"Jim," he said abruptly, "do you believe it was Cale took a shot at you through the window that night in the Montezuma?"

"For a while it looked a bit that way to me," Grant replied. "To all appearances, Whitmer was the logical suspect. He had a motive — revenge for the thrashing he got that night. And unless I'm mistaken, Whitmer is left-handed."

"He is," nodded Sanchez.

"And the man who fired that shot fired it with his left hand."

Sanchez whistled. "Looks rather like an open-and-shut case against Cale," he commented.

"So it appeared to me, until the other night," Grant conceded. "I'll tell you why I changed my mind."

He regaled the ranch owner with an account of Lafe Haskins' attempt to drygulch him and what had followed.

"The night I was shot at in the Montezuma, I thought of Haskins," he concluded, "but when it began to appear Haskins had not come to Laredo, that left only Whitmer to be considered. But when I recognized the man talking with Whispering Shane the other night as Haskins, I became inclined to discount Whitmer. Very probably Haskins would have shot with his left hand that night."

"And you cut off his trigger finger!" Sanchez repeated.

"Yes, and I was rather ashamed of myself right afterward; it was an ugly thing to do."

"You should have cut his throat!" Camera growled. "But where does that leave Whitmer — associating with such characters?"

"I don't know," Grant admitted. "But remember, we have no proof that Shane has anything to do with the wide-looping, nor Haskins either, for that matter."

"No, we have no proof, but as Jess Sanborn would say, I've a right to my notions," Sanchez grunted.

"And Whitmer might have a perfectly legitimate reason for dealing with Shane," Grant continued. "I understand Shane has large and diversified business interests."

"Yes, he has," conceded Sanchez, "but what business Whitmer could have with him I can't conceive, and I'm willing to bet that whatever it is, it will mean trouble."

Camera glanced out the window at the sound of hoof-beats.

"Here comes Lila," he said. "Now I wonder where that imp has been gallivanting off to?"

A moment later the girl entered the room. Her eyes brightened as they rested on Jim Grant.

"Hello," she greeted him. "I was beginning to think you'd forgotten us."

"Impossible!" he returned emphatically.

"Nice of you to say so, even if you don't mean it," she said.

"Where you been?" asked Camera.

"Oh, just riding down to the southwest," she replied carelessly but with a dancing light in her big eyes.

112

"All right, out with it!" growled Camera. "What have you been up to? You look like a cat that's just lapped a saucer of cream and sees the canary's cage open."

The dimple was prominent at the corner of her red mouth as she replied with apparent irrelevance. "I met Cale Whitmer over by our west wire."

"The devil you did!" Exclaimed Camera. "What did he have to say?"

"Oh, he was nice to me, as usual," she answered.

Jim Grant felt vaguely irritated at the thought of Cale Whitmer being "nice" to her, and immediately wondered why.

"Yes, he was nice," Lila repeated. "As I said once before, I guess he considers there's no sense in including the Sanchez women in his silly feud with you. A pity Norma doesn't feel the same way, in reverse."

"Norma has always been friendly enough towards you, hasn't she?" said Camera.

"Oh, sure, she's always been friendly enough with *me*," Lila replied with meaningful emphasis.

Camera flushed a little, set his jaw and said nothing.

"Isn't it time to eat?" Lila asked plaintively. "I'm starved."

"Should be ready any minute," Camera replied. "I'll go tell the cook to rattle his hocks."

He left the room. Lila waited a moment, then turned to Grant.

"Jim," she said, "I'm going to tell you something I didn't mention to Cam, because I have no desire to fan the flames any hotter than they are right now. If I tell him, he'll hit the ceiling, but I feel I've got to tell somebody because — well, it's rather peculiar. As I said, I ran into Cale Whitmer this afternoon. Or rather he ran into me, as he has a habit of doing whenever he gets the chance. He looked very, very pleased about something. And," she hesitated a moment, "he asked me to marry him, for the second time in the past month."

Jim Grant's eyes widened and he gulped. "And what did you say?" The question was out before he had time to realize it was decidedly personal.

Lila looked him squarely in the eyes. "I told him I wouldn't," she replied. Grant experienced a sudden feeling of intense relief.

"The first time he asked me was quite a while ago, before his father died," the girl went on. "That time I didn't know him as well as I do now and I rather liked him. I didn't say yes, but I didn't say no. The second time was about a month ago, when I met him over to the east, on what's now your holding. That time I told him I couldn't even consider it with him and Uncle Cam on the outs like they were.

"That," she added reminiscently, "was just before you folks showed up in the section."

"The row between him and Camera is still going strong," Grant remarked, "so naturally you would say no."

The ghost of a smile touched her red lips. "Of course," she replied. "What other reason would there be for me saying no?"

Grant was at a loss for an appropriate answer. The smile became a little more than a ghost; instantly she was grave. She cast a quick glance at the door leading to the dining room and spoke hurriedly.

"But what I've just said merely leads up to what I really have to tell you," she said, lowering her voice; "what I don't want Cam to know, not at the present at least. It was Cale's reaction when I said no for the third time. He just smiled, a rather malicious kind of a smile. I'd say the word gloating describes it better than any other. He smiled and said, 'I expect the next time I ask you, you'll be glad to say yes.' I asked him what the devil he meant, but he just smiled again, the same cat-and-mouse sort of smile, waved his hand and rode away."

"I wonder what he meant," said Grant.

"I have no idea, but his expression worried me," Lila replied. "He seemed so darn sure of himself. I can't think of anything that would cause me to change my mind, but I'm worried."

At that moment, Camera Sanchez was heard leaving the kitchen. Lila put a finger to her lips to enjoin silence, and the conversation ended.

"All set to go," Camera said as he entered the room. "Let's eat."

During the course of the meal, the talk got around to the stolen cattle and Grant's fruitless endeavour to learn where they went and how. Lila suddenly made a suggestion that Grant thought worthy of consideration.

"Jim," she said, "did you ever think that they might leave the hills to the north of where you kept watch, head east and reach the river farther downstream?"

115

"No, I never did," Grant admitted thoughtfully. "Maybe they could do that."

"Oh, sure they could reach the river that way, but they'd have the devil of a time getting across with the water at flood stage as it's been for weeks," Camera said. "Up this way is bad enough — I have my doubts they could do it south of the hills where you were holed up, although possibly it could be done — but farther down the river is narrower and a lot deeper. They'd have to go halfway to Brownsville before they'd find a place they could cross."

Grant nodded and didn't argue the point, but just the same Lila's chance remark had set him to thinking. The cows went somewhere, and he had just about exhausted all other possibilities. Perhaps Camera could be mistaken; there might be a hidden ford similar to the Indian Crossing at Laredo.

He regretted that he had no further chance for a word in private with Lila before leaving the hacienda; but he was anxious to get back to the Swinging J. So, declining urgent invitations to spend the night, he rode away through the deepening dusk.

CHAPTER
EIGHTEEN

It was late when Grant reached the Swinging J ranch-house; everybody had gone to bed. He gave Smoke a good rubdown, a generous helping of oats and water with a little whiskey in it. From the kitchen he secured a store of staple provisions which he packed in his saddle pouches. After making sure his Winchester and Colts were in perfect working order, he repaired to the ranch house and smoked and rested for a couple of hours. The hours after midnight found him in the saddle again, riding east by south at a good pace.

Dawn was breaking when he sighted the south spur of the hills. He did not approach them but veered south until he reached the north bank of the Rio Grande. Full day had broken, and in the strengthening light he rode slowly along the bank, where the ground was soft and there was little or no grass. He observed with satisfaction that Smoke's irons cut deep in the soil; nothing could pass this way without leaving evidence of its passing.

Mile after mile he rode, with the hurrying waters of the Rio Grande on his right and the endless sweep of the brush country to his left.

He had covered nearly twenty miles and the sun was nearing the zenith when he abruptly pulled the moros to a halt and sat staring at the ground ahead. It was very soft at the water's edge and cut by a multitude of hoof marks, among which were the prints of horses' irons.

Straight to the water's edge ran the deep scorings, and there they stopped.

Here, to all appearances, was a bovine similar to the lemmings of Norway, the little rodents that migrate by the thousands to the sea to plunge in and perish.

But cows didn't do that; they had to be shoved into water. And the cow never lived that could swim the Rio Grande here in its present state of flood.

"But if they didn't go into the water, where the devil did they go?" Grant demanded angrily of Smoke. "Well, I'm going to find out if I have to stay here all summer."

This was the brush country, and there was plenty of concealment for horse and man. Grant hunted out a favourable spot in the heart of a thicket, from where he could see the river bank for some distance in both directions. He took the rig off the moros and turned him loose to graze. Collecting very dry wood, he made a tiny fire and cooked some breakfast, taking the chance that the small amount of smoke would not be observed. After eating, he spread his blanket and lay down to sleep, knowing that Smoke would not stray from the thicket and that his warning snort would give the alarm if anybody approached his hiding place.

He awoke at sundown. First he led the moros to the river's edge and allowed him to drink his fill. Then as twilight deepened he rekindled his fire, knowing the smoke would not been seen in the dusk, and cooked and ate. After a leisurely cigarette he settled down to watch and wait.

The night passed without incident and so did the following day, but Grant had grimly resolved to keep his lonely vigil until something happened or hunger drove him forth. Hour after hour he lay in the star-burned dark. Midnight came and went, and he was thoroughly disgusted with the whole monotonous business. Then gradually he became conscious of an alien sound, a pulsing murmur that slowly grew louder until it became the steady beat of a paddle wheel and the noise of a steamer's exhaust. Grant listened idly; doubtless one of the small trading steamers that plied the Mexican villages on the south bank and bore a miscellaneous cargo to Brownsville or Port Isabel.

Louder and louder grew the beat of the paddles and the grumble of the exhaust; then abruptly the sounds ceased for a moment, resumed again, much closer, kept up for another moment or two and again ceased. Grant, watching from the outer fringe of the growth, suddenly saw a huge shape loom in the starlight reflected from the river. It drifted slowly toward the north bank and came to rest with a gentle thudding and bumping; the steamer was nosing the bank.

Then abruptly he heard another sound, a sound that set every nerve to tingling — the distant bleat of a weary and disgusted steer. He strained his ears to make certain he had not been mistaken.

It came again. Jim Grant whistled soundlessly behind his teeth. Tense, alert, every faculty at hair trigger, he waited.

Lights flashed on the steamer. Grant could see shadowy figures moving about her deck. A sound as of the winding of a great clock drifted up to him from the water, the clank of a turning windlass. There was a rattling of chains, a creaking and grinding. A broad section of the vessel's side opened out and was slowly lowered until its upper edge rested on the bank. More lights appeared, and more shadowy figures. Straining his eyes, Grant could see that the lowered section made a broad gangway into the steamer's hull.

The bawling of the approaching cattle grew louder; Grant could now hear the patter of their hoofs on the trail and the metallic clicking of horses' irons. Five more minutes and the murky bulk of the herd hove into view. Grant estimated there was somewhere between sixty and seventy head, and a moment later the gleam of the lanterns showed them to be prime beef stock. He wished he could have read the brands, but in the gloom that was impossible. And the faces of the rustlers were only whitish blurs.

The point men converged on the herd, crowding the leaders together as they slackened speed. Bellowing protest, the steers were shoved onto the "gangplank". Their hoofs clattered on the steel plates, thudded as they disappeared into the yawning cavern of the vessel's hold. With swing and flank riders crowding in and the drag surging forward, the whole herd was loaded onto the steamer in a matter of minutes.

A hoarse command sounded from the boat's deck, the clanking of the windlass was heard, and the hinged section of the steamer's side slowly rose to clang shut. The horses of the rustlers bunched at the water's edge, and some low-voiced conversation ensued. Another shout from the wheelhouse, and the noise of the exhaust and the slapping of the paddles vibrated on the night air. The vessel fell away from the shore and, with no lights burning, ploughed downstream and was quickly lost to sight. The horsemen, a dozen or more in number, wheeled their horses, rode swiftly back the way they had come and vanished. Jim Grant relaxed, expelling the breath he had unconsciously been holding. So that was how it was done! Abruptly he recalled Camera Sanchez mentioning that, among his other activities, Whispering Shane owned an interest in several small steamboats that plied between Rio Grande City and Brownsville. He waited until he was sure the rustlers had departed; then he put the rig on Smoke and rode swiftly westwards along the river's edge.

It was almost noon when Grant reached the Swinging J ranch house. Old Joel was on the porch, and greeted him with a shout.

"Where have you been, Jim?" The owner asked. "You look as if you'd been making a night of it."

"I have," Grant replied. "Tell the cook to rustle me some hot coffee and something to eat, and I'll tell you."

When Grant had finished recounting his experiences, Joel swore in wrathful amazement.

"Water-runnin' wide-loopers, that's a new one!" he sputtered. "What are we going to do about it?"

"We're going to do our best to bust up that gang of thieves once and for all," Grant replied grimly.

"You mean ride down there and lay for 'em?"

"Guess that's the general idea," Grant said.

Old Joel tugged his moustache thoughtfully. "Think we'd better notify the sheriff and have the law with us?" he suggested.

Grant shook his head. "I thought of that," he admitted, "but decided against it. I'm pretty much of the opinion that a close tab is kept on the sheriff. If he was seen riding out here with a posse, very likely the word would be passed along and the hellions would hole up for a spell. No, I think we'd better go it on our own."

"How about letting Sanchez in on it? He's sort of interested."

"Same objection applies," Grant answered. "Sanchez and his men may be watched, also."

"Reckon you're right," Joel acceded. "Going to make it tomorrow night?"

Grant again shook his head. "I doubt if they'd run another herd tomorrow night, even if they've got one at a holding spot somewhere. Day after tomorrow night will be better. We'll leave here three or four hours before daylight to minimize any chance of being spotted. We'll have to hole up part of the day in the brush, but there's plenty of cover, and it's most unlikely that a watch is kept down there. Now I'm going to have something to eat and then lie down for a while; I'm all in."

"Okay," said Collison, "I'll round up the boys and give them the lowdown. Going to take everybody, I suppose?"

"Everybody that can ride," Grant answered. "There's a dozen of the hellions, maybe more; we'll need all the guns we've got. And we've got to get the jump on them or it's liable to be too bad for us. That's a bunch that'll stop at nothing."

"I predict they'll stop, down there on the river bank, and stay stopped," Joel said grimly.

Two nights later, under a lowering sky, the grim posse rode east by south. Every man was armed with a six-gun and rifle and itching for a chance to use them. Grant knew that Collison, Zeke Crowley, old Gene Kelton and one or two others were excellent shots, and while the remainder of the Swinging J hands were mediocre or a bit worse, with the element of surprise in their favour, he was sanguine as to the results of a brush with the outlaws.

"But we've got to get the jump on them," he cautioned his men. "Give them a chance to get set and we're in for trouble. We must be all over them before they tumble to what's going on. Don't underestimate them; they're dangerous men and have nothing to lose by fighting to a finish. For them it'll be just a matter of choosing between hot lead and a rope, and they're not liable to choose the rope if there's any way of escaping it."

Before dawn, the posse had passed the southern tip of the hills, and Grant breathed easier. There was always the chance that somebody might be posted on that natural watchtower from which anything happening on the Swinging J range could be observed. Now he had little fear of detection. They would hole up in the brush near where the trail of the stolen cows reached the water. Then it would be but a matter of waiting and watching.

All the long afternoon the Swinging J hands remained undercover.

At dusk, he took a chance and lighted some small fires and cooked something to eat. Food and steaming coffee and the coolness of the evening put the hands in a better frame of mind, but did not lessen their desire to wreak vengeance on the outlaws.

Full darkness fell, and the posse settled down to wait.

It was a long wait and a tedious one. Nerves tightened and imagination ran riot. Time and again somebody was sure he had heard something, but it always turned out to be a false alarm. Dawn drew near, and Grant was beginning to fear they were destined to spend another day of discomfort in the brush. Then gradually he became aware of the familiar pulsing murmur that grew to the sputter of an exhaust and the beat of a paddle wheel.

"Here comes the steamer," he told the others. "Things should happen soon."

"Going to hit them before they load the cows?" Collison asked.

124

"No, they'll be scattered then," Grant replied. "After they get the cattle aboard they'll be bunched. When the last cow is loaded will be the time. Listen, didn't I hear a steer bawl a long way off?"

"You did," Collison replied a moment later. "There it is again."

"They're coming," said Grant. "Everybody at the edge of the brush here, now, where you can see the landing. I hope the horses keep quiet."

"We muffled all the bit irons after we got the rigs on them," Zeke Crowley said. "Should be okay if one of 'em don't take a notion to sing a song to the stars — they're good at that just before daylight. Maybe it woulda been better to lead 'em way off into the brush."

"I thought of that, but we might need them if some of the hellions get away," Grant replied. "So I figured to take a chance and have them ready close to hand. Better stop talking now; sounds travel a long way on a still night, and there might be somebody riding ahead of the herd for some reason or other."

Silence fell, broken only by the sound of the approaching steamer and the more distinct bawling of the cattle as they drew nearer.

The shadowy bulk of the steamer loomed in the starlight. She nosed to shore; the "gangplank" was dropped. Lights flashed on her deck and gleamed through the opening in her side. The bleating of the approaching cattle was much louder, and a moment later the beat of their hoofs on the trail could be made out.

"Get set," Grant whispered. "Wait till I give the word before you start shooting."

On came the herd, grumbling and bawling their protest at being hurried down the rocky trail. The air was filled with the stench of their sweat and quivered to the clashing of horns. Rough voices shouted and the point men surged in, crowding the leaders together as the herd slackened speed. Another moment and hoofs were thudding on the "gangplank".

This herd was bigger than the last; fully a hundred head, Grant estimated. He stood tense and alert as the last shaggy back vanished inside the hull. The rustlers clumped together on the bank, some twelve or fourteen of them, their horses blowing. Rough jests were shouted and answered in kind by the men on the steamer's deck. Grant opened his lips to give the word to cut loose. And at that moment one of the horses decided to neigh.

The outlaws whirled in their saddles at the sound, uttering startled exclamations.

"Let them have it!" Grant roared, and began shooting with both hands. A crashing volley sounded, then the steady crackling of the cowboys' guns.

Under that hail of lead, the outlaw group seemed to dissolve. Men fell from their horses, screaming and groaning. Those remaining in the saddle jerked their guns and fired wildly. Grant heard a curse on his right and knew somebody was hit. A slug fanned his face; another turned his hat sideways on his head. A third grazed the flesh of his left arm. He stuffed cartridges into his empty guns and blazed away as fast as he could

126

pull trigger. Riderless horses were streaking away in every direction, and abruptly he realized there was nothing more to shoot at.

On the steamer's deck the windlass was clanking furiously. The lowered section of plates was slowly rising.

"Don't let that boat get away!" Grant shouted, and rushed forward, the cowboys streaming after him.

But the captain of the steamer was a man of daring. With a quarter of his vessel's side wide open to nearly water level, he bawled an order. The exhaust boomed; the paddles beat the water to foam. Grant fired at the wheelhouse again and again. A wailing curse echoed the reports, but the boat lurched away from the shore, her exhaust bellowing, the windlass clamouring. With lead smacking her sides and whistling over her deck, she lurched on. The full grip of the current caught her, and an instant later she vanished in the gloom. The crackle of her exhaust and the beat of her paddles came back mockingly through the dark.

"If we could just get word to Rio Grande City they'd grab her there," Collison shouted.

"Not a chance," Grant replied. "She'll get rid of the cows long before she reaches the town, and there'll be no evidence against her, even if we could get there ahead of her, which we can't. Let's see what we bagged."

The cowboys, guns ready for action, hurried to where the bodies lay sprawled on the ground, shot to pieces. Two were still breathing, but their lives were draining out through their shattered lungs and they were unconscious.

"Here's one that ain't dead yet," called Crowley. "Come here, Jim."

Grant stooped beside the desperately wounded outlaw, a lean and cadaverous individual with carroty red hair. Glazing eyes glared up into his.

"You're taking the Big Jump, fellow," Grant said. "Why not make it easier for yourself and tell us who's back of this hellishness?"

The fixed eyes still glared. The rustler gurgled through the blood in his throat. His chest arched mightily as he fought for air, fell in and did not rise again. Jim Grant stood up and shook his head.

"Mean and bad to the last, but with plenty of guts," was his requiem for the dead outlaw. "How many did we get altogether?"

"An even dozen," replied Gene Kelton.

"But a couple got away," Crowley exclaimed excitedly. "I saw them streaking it back up the trail. I figure one was shot up — he was wobbling in the hull. Big fellers, both of 'em, with whiskers."

Jim Grant glanced to the east. There the sky was rosy and the light was quickly strengthening.

"Get your horse," he told Crowley, "and bring mine along. We'll try and run those hellions down, or maybe at least trail them to their hangout — they must have one somewhere."

Crowley rushed away. Old Joel turned to Grant with an anxious face.

"Don't you think the rest of us had better go with you?" He asked. "Those are desperate men."

"I think Zeke and I can handle them," Grant replied as Crowley drew rein beside them, leading Smoke. "Our horses are a good deal the best in the bunch, and I believe we'll have a better chance of running them down than if everybody went along. Be seeing you, Uncle Joel."

He swung into the saddle, and he and Crowley charged up the trail. The cowboys watched them go, then turned for a closer examination of the bodies.

CHAPTER
NINETEEN

For two hours, Grant and Crowley rode at a swift pace. The sun was well up, and it was becoming very hot; both men and horses were sweating freely. Ahead loomed the rugged bulk of the low hills, now quite close.

"Look out!" Crowley suddenly exclaimed, dragging his mount to a sliding halt. "There's a horse standing beside the trail!"

"And there's a man lying *in* the trail," Grant added.

For tense minutes they sat watching, and scanning the surrounding terrain. But the man never moved, nor did the horse, which stood with head hanging and one forefoot raised. They rode cautiously forward and pulled up beside the body.

The man lay on his back, his eyes wide open and seeming to stare up at the hot sun. His shaggy dark beard was blood-stained, and blow flies were swarming over his face.

"Good God! What happened to him?" Ejaculated Crowley. "Did his horse fall with him?"

"Don't think so," Grant replied soberly. "I'd say the horse over there belonged to his partner. It must have gone lame, and the other hellion needed this fellow's

130

cayuse to make sure of his own getaway. So he knocked him out and then beat him to death with a gun barrel."

"The snake-blooded hydrophobia skunk!" Exploded Crowley.

"Yes, he's all of that," Grant agreed grimly. There was little doubt in his mind as to the identity of the second bearded man who had made his escape from the scene of the fight. What lay before them bore all the earmarks of being Lafe Haskins' handiwork.

Crowley dismounted and examined the injured horse. "Just a sprain; no bones broken," he called.

"Take off the rig, and he'll make out till we can send somebody to pick him up," Grant said. "Wearing a brand?"

"Mexican skillet-of-snakes burn," grunted Crowley. "Don't mean anything." He divested the horse of saddle and bridle, gave the hurt leg a little rubbing. The animal blew softly through his nose and seemed to appreciate what was done for him. As Crowley straightened up, he hobbled aside a few paces and began nibbling grass.

"Let's go," Grant said. "Maybe we can catch up with the hellion, though I doubt it. Chances are we'll lose his trail in the hills."

That was just what happened. On the hill crest the fugitive's tracks left those made by the cattle and turned into a rocky ravine. Grant and Crowley followed them for some distance but lost them on the stony ground. The ravine was cut by other gorges and gullies, and it was impossible to tell which way their quarry had turned. Finally they gave up in disgust and headed back to the river.

When they arrived at the scene of the fight they found the outlaws' horses had been rounded up. The well trained animals, after their initial fright, had halted a short distance away and were easily caught. A couple of slightly wounded cowboys had been patched up and a meal cooked. Grant and Crowley ate heartily, and between mouthfuls retailed the results of their pursuit of the two fugitives. Or rather, as Grant expressed it, the lack of results.

"Well, anyhow, one more was taken care of," commented Collison. "That makes thirteen — unlucky thirteen for them. Now what?"

"To Laredo to hand the sheriff our bag," said Grant. "He's liable to give us the devil for not notifying him of what was in the wind, but I expect he'll get over it, especially if some of those devils are recognized and tie up with somebody else. That's what I'm hoping for."

The bodies were roped to the saddles of the outlaws' horses, and the grisly caravan set out for Laredo.

It was long past dark when they arrived at the river town, but there were still plenty of people on the streets who stared in astonishment as Grant and his men made for the sheriff's office. A crowd quickly gathered, constantly augmented by new arrivals. The air was a-whirl with oaths and exclamations and wild conjecture as to just what had happened.

Sheriff Foster tugged his moustache and shook his grizzled head as he listened to Grant's story.

"Looks like you sort of took the law in your own hands, Grant, but I reckon you were justified," he said when the tale was finished. "Anyhow, the section owes you a vote of thanks for ridding it of those pests. Bring 'em in and stretch 'em out on the floor and we'll see if anybody knows them."

The dead rustlers were laid out on their backs. A long line of the morbidly curious began filing past the bodies. There were also a number of bartenders and tradespeople hastily summoned by the sheriff. Several barkeeps were positive they had served one or another of the dead men at some time, but were otherwise vague about them. The same went for others who thought they recognized some of the rigid faces. Nobody could come up with any really definite information.

Finally Sheriff Foster gave up in disgust. "Same old story," he growled to Grant. "Nobody knows from nothing, or if they do they ain't talking. All right; everybody outside. Bert," he ordered a deputy, "go notify the undertaker and the coroner. Maybe old Doc will want to hold an inquest tomorrow. No sense in it, but the law says it should be done."

When the crowd had departed, he shut the door and turned to Grant.

"And you say they were loading the cows onto a steamer? That's a new one. Been done over to the west of here, with scows, but I don't recall it ever being done with a steamboat before. A pity you couldn't have grabbed that boat; then we should have been able to tie them up definitely with somebody. Hmmm! I wonder."

"I'm wondering a bit, too," Grant replied quietly.

"You *could* be right," was the sheriff's cryptic answer, "but I expect we'd have considerable trouble making our 'wonderings' stand up in court. This town polls enough votes to swing any county or legislative election."

Grant nodded his understanding. He had gathered from Camera Sanchez' remarks that Whispering Shane wielded political influence that not only carried weight with local officials but extended to the capital in Austin.

"Well, you thinned out their bunch quite a bit, anyhow," said Foster. "I've a notion they ain't got many left kicking."

"Perhaps, but the head of the outfit is still running around loose, in my opinion, and that sort of a head grows another body fast," Grant replied gloomily.

Neither Grant nor Collison was in a mood for entertainment, so they had something to eat and went to bed.

The coroner's jury verdict the following morning was typically cow country. It said, in effect, that the varmints had it coming, and Grant and the Swinging J outfit were commended for doing a good chore.

After the inquest, Grant rounded up the hands and rode back to the Swinging J.

Camera Sanchez was sitting in the room that served him as an office, taking care of some book work, when Bert Trimble, Sheriff Foster's chief deputy, rode up to the hacienda.

"Why, hello, Bert," Sanchez greeted him as the deputy entered. "What brings you here? Going to throw us all in jail?"

"Nope," Trimble replied soberly, "but I got some papers to serve on you, Camera."

"Now what?" Sanchez asked. "Somebody suing me for a bill one of my tenants didn't pay?"

"Nope," Trimble repeated. "Cale Whitmer is bringing a suit against you. Here are the papers; read 'em."

Sanchez' eyes widened with astonishment as he perused the document. Stripped of legal verbiage, it charged that Camera Sanchez and those before him had unlawfully occupied the land known as the Rafter S Ranch without right of legal tenancy and asked that the land in question be declared state land and open to the public for purchase.

Sanchez looked up from the document and stared at Trimble. "Has Cale Whitmer gone plumb loco?" he demanded. "He knows very well the land is and always has been held by right of a grant from the Spanish King to my grandfather, Tomas Sanchez, and that the courts have consistently held those grants to be valid."

"I don't know anything about it, Camera," Trimble replied. "My chore was just to serve the papers."

"Of course," Sanchez acceded. "Okay, I'll look into it. I always figured Cale Whitmer to be crazy as any bedbug that ever walked down a sheet, and now I know it. Come on and have something to eat, Bert."

"Got to get back to the office," Trimble declined. "Hope you don't have any trouble, Camera."

"Don't worry; I won't," Sanchez assured him.

After the deputy had gone, Camera Sanchez laughed heartily at the whole ludicrous affair. But he didn't laugh a little later, when he opened the drawer in which the old grant had always been kept. The ancient document was not there, although Camera was positive he had never removed it from its resting place of years.

The house was ransacked from top to bottom, but the all-important parchment was not found. Camera saddled up and rode to Laredo to consult with his lawyer, Judge Parkinson. In a few words he laid the case before the jurist.

The judge read the papers carefully, removed his spectacles and regarded Camera very seriously.

"And you can't find the original grant? Camera, without that grant or strong corroborative evidence to show it was actually received by your grandfather, you are in trouble."

"But, Judge," Camera exploded, "I've lived on that land all my life, and so did my father before me."

"True," conceded the judge, "but long occupancy alone does not in itself confer title. That's been thrashed out in the courts. Time and again, cattlemen who occupied open range and claimed it have had their claims refuted. This suit implies that you are in the nature of a squatter on state land and prays that you be designated as such and evicted from said land."

Camera Sanchez wet his suddenly dry lips with his tongue. "And do you think Whitmer has a case?" he asked.

"I'm not prepared to give a definite opinion as yet, but unless you can produce the grant or evidence satisfactory to the courts that it was issued, it looks that way to me."

"But what has Whitmer to gain from this, if he puts it over?" Sanchez demanded. "The land wouldn't be deeded to him; it would, as that paper says, be declared state land open to purchase."

"And the land office would most certainly grant you priority," said the lawyer. "But — would you have or be able to raise the money to buy the land if it was put up for sale?"

"You know enough of my affairs to know very well I couldn't," growled Camera. "So far as ready money is concerned, I'm broke and in debt. Does Whitmer aim to buy up the land, if he can get away with this?"

The lawyer shook his head. "Very unlikely, I'd say," he replied. "I know something of Whitmer's affairs, too, and I'm confident he is in no position to make such a purchase. He couldn't get the money with his ranch for security; the banks wouldn't touch it. For Whitmer's title to a large part of the land he claims is a bit shaky, also. No bank would put out that amount of money against a dubious title."

"Then who the devil is back of this?" demanded Camera. "That is, if you don't believe Whitmer is doing it on his own."

"That is something I'd like to find out," Parkinson answered dryly, "and I'm liable to have trouble doing it. Whoever it is — oh yes, I'm convinced somebody is backing Whitmer — is a shrewd and farsighted individual and is liable to have his tracks well covered."

Camera stood up.

"Okay, Judge," he said, "but just the same I think I'll ride over and have a little talk with *amigo* Whitmer."

"No! No!" protested the lawyer. "Having a row with Whitmer right now would prejudice your claim. No good would come of it, and you'd just play into the hands of whoever is back of all this. I want you to promise me that you will stay away from Whitmer so long as he makes no overt move that would justify intervention. Otherwise I'll have nothing to do with the business."

"All right," Sanchez agreed reluctantly. "I promise, but he'd better keep out of my way."

"First I'll play for time," Judge Parkinson said. "The longer we can postpone a hearing, the more chance we'll have to dig up something to support your claim."

It was characteristic of Camera that he should think of others before himself.

"What bothers me most is what will happen to my small tenant farmers, many of whom have lived on the property all their lives," he said. "Old Joel Collison bought from me in good faith and, I know, just about stripped himself of ready money to do so. I don't think Collison would be in any better position to pay for his holdings a second time than I am to put down the required money for mine."

"Don't worry too much," said the lawyer. "I haven't lost many cases in the course of my legal career, and I hope not to lose this one. Just take it easy and go about your business as usual."

"I suppose I'd better tell Collison about it," Camera suggested.

"Yes, that's best," said Parkinson. "Perhaps he can be of help, and also that young range boss of his who did such a fine chore of thinning out the outlaw bunch. He's shrewd and resourceful. Yes, take them both into your confidence and withhold nothing. No telling what Grant might be able to do."

CHAPTER
TWENTY

Camera Sanchez left the attorney's office with a heavy heart. He dreaded the chore just ahead of him, but he steeled his resolution and headed for the Swinging J ranch house. He had to tell Joel Collison and Jim Grant what had happened, and he might as well get it over with as quickly as possible. Delay would only serve to make the task harder.

The interview turned out to be much less painful than Camera anticipated. After he had finished relating what had taken place, his hearers sat for a moment in stunned silence. Then old Joel shrugged his scrawny shoulders.

"Well, I started out with nothing, and if I end up with nothing I guess I can stand it," he said. "Anyhow, we still have enough cattle to get a start in a small way some place else, eh, Jim?"

"You're right," Grant nodded, "but maybe it won't come to that. We won't give up without a fight. Camera, you say the grant was always kept in that particular drawer you mentioned?"

"That's right," Sanchez agreed.

"Was the drawer kept locked?"

"Why, no," Camera said. "In fact, I never attached any particular value to the thing; regarded it as a sort of heirloom, as it were."

"And when did you see it last?"

"About a year ago, when old Shadrach Naylor, who had been Dad's friend, came over from Arizona for a visit. Somehow we got to talking about my grandfather — Naylor knew him, too — and that brought up the subject of the grant. I hauled it out and showed it to him."

"I see," Grant said thoughtfully. "And who besides Naylor was present at the time?"

"I really couldn't say," Sanchez replied. "Several of the boys were in the room, of that I'm sure, although just who besides Jess Sanborn and old Prouty and Bill Hogadorn I don't recall. Quite a few of the older hands knew Naylor and dropped in to say hello to him. There's almost always somebody in the living room, for that matter. It's a sort of general loafing place and always has been."

"And whoever was present would have known you took the paper from the drawer in your office?"

"Sure," Sanchez admitted. "The office is right off the living room, and with the door open anybody could look in and see where I got it."

"I see," Grant repeated. "I'd say the paper was deliberately stolen rather than misplaced."

"But who in the devil would steal it, and why?" Camera asked.

"The first half of the question I can't answer," Grant conceded, "but an answer to the second half isn't hard to find. Somebody must have recognized the value of the original signed approval of the grant and understood what would happen if you couldn't produce it at such a time as this. Somebody looked ahead and saw opportunity."

"You trying to tell me that one of my hands would be able to figure that out?" Demanded Sanchez. "They're just an average lot of punchers, and I'd say such a thing was beyond them."

"Perhaps," Grant replied dryly. "Can you always vouch for every man who works for you? And are you always familiar with his background?"

"Of course not," Sanchez was forced to admit. "There's always a certain turnover in the cow business, as you know. I've had men I hired during the busy season who only stayed with me a matter of months or weeks."

"Exactly." Grant nodded. "Looks like you may have hired one who was a bit more than he appeared to be. Or maybe he was planted with you by somebody for the purpose of obtaining the approval signed by the Spanish King and countersigned by Jose de Escandon, his colonizer."

"But that sounds fantastic," protested Sanchez.

"This whole business seems fantastic, on the surface, but recent developments tend to prove it an unpleasantly substantial reality," Grant countered.

"Unfortunately, I'm afraid you're right," Sanchez acceded. "But what I'd like to know is who is back of this. Parkinson says he is convinced that Cale Whitmer has neither the ingenuity nor the legal knowledge to have formulated such a scheme and that somebody with a mighty good legal brain promoted it. Not the lawyer who drew up the papers — he's just an average practitioner, Parkinson said."

Jim Grant nodded without replying. He had a pretty good notion who was responsible, although he preferred not to mention it at the moment. Doubtless Whispering Shane was the prime mover now that the affair was under way, but the project had been hatched in Lafe Haskins' shrewd, half crazed legal mind. Shane and Haskins, very probably playing on Whitmer's hatred of Camera Sanchez, had been able to persuade the Bradded R owner to bring the suit, thus giving it legal and ethical responsibility.

Camera said goodbye a little later and headed back to his hacienda. Grant and Collison discussed the matter at length, exploring all angles without arriving at a satisfactory conclusion.

Judge Parkinson carefully planned his campaign of delay, but when he moved to put it into execution, he encountered unexpected opposition. The general desire of the courts and the land office appeared to be to wind up the business as quickly as possible. He did manage to wring certain concessions for his client, for the judge was a shrewd practitioner and not to be lightly disregarded, but far fewer than he had hoped for.

Parkinson was not without political acumen. He did a little quiet investigating and learned that word had gone out from the capital hinting that speed would be appreciated.

"Somebody pulled a few wires," he confided to Jim Grant, who had dropped in to talk with him.

"Naturally," Grant replied. "Didn't you expect that?"

"It didn't come altogether as a surprise," the judge conceded. "It was logical to believe that they would lay the groundwork before bringing the suit. But who did the pulling?"

Grant looked the lawyer straight in the eye. "Who do you think?" He asked softly.

Judge Parkinson hesitated, studying Grant shrewdly. Grant answered the question for him.

"Whispering Shane, of course; who else?"

"I think you're right," the attorney returned meditatively. "Only I'd never have given Shane credit for the legal knowledge necessary to evolve such a scheme. I'd never have believed he had it."

"He hasn't," Grant replied tersely.

"No? Then who has?" asked Parkinson.

It was Grant's turn to hesitate, but only for a moment. Briefly he related what he knew of Lafe Haskins and his recent activity. The judge pursed his lips in a soundless whistle.

"And you think he was mixed up in the cattle stealing too?" He asked.

"I do," Grant answered. "In fact, I'm certain of it."

"And he's been associating with Shane?"

"Yes, and presumably with Whitmer also."

"Then if we could grab Haskins for something illegal, we'd have the other two where the hair's short."

"Sure, if we could grab him," Grant conceded, "but how? I have no proof that Haskins took part in the rustling or the killings. I didn't see him, and all Zeke Crowley saw down by the river were two big men with whiskers. Crowley could not identify either of those men as Haskins."

"How about the two attempts on your life?" Asked the lawyer. "We might be able to hold him on that and perhaps get something out of him."

"Exactly the same difficulty obtains there; no proof," Grant said. "Just as I am convinced in my own mind that Haskins is mixed up in the rustling, so am I convinced that he twice tried to kill me; but I can't prove it. Up there on the hillside? Haskins could swear he was just waiting to get a shot at a deer and that I came along and wantonly assaulted him. The shot through the window? I didn't see anybody, nor did anyone else. I could swear that a left-handed man pulled the trigger and assume that Haskins would have shot left-handed because of his injured right hand. But there are lots of left-handed folks, including Cale Whitmer, who at the moment certainly didn't have cause to love me. See how it stands? We have nothing on Haskins, no matter what we may think."

"A tough customer, all right," the judge agreed soberly, "in the same category, it would appear, as Garland Shane. Nobody has ever been able to get anything on Shane. We had a grand jury barking around his hole once, but nothing came of it."

"So, everything considered, how does it look?" asked Grant.

"It looks bad," growled Parkinson. "Unless Camera Sanchez can bring forward some corroborative evidence to show that grant was approved, and bring it forward fast, the court and the land office are going to rule against him. There's no doubt but that the trial judge is leaning toward Whitmer and liable to go along with anything he requests or is told to request by Shane or Haskins. The judge is honest enough, but he's up for re-election, and Whispering Shane can swing a lot of votes."

"Not a very promising prospect, but something may turn up before the trial date," Grant nodded. "Well, I'll be seeing you, Judge; I'm going to ride up and have a talk with Camera."

Camera was not in evidence when he reached the hacienda; Lila met him at the door.

"Come on in," she said. "Cam's at the stables. I want to talk to you a minute before he shows up."

Grant entered and sat down. Lila remained standing, regarding him with a strained expression.

"Jim," she said, "I received a note that I know was from Cale Whitmer this morning. A man gave it to one of our tenant farmers to bring to me. One of Cale's riders, I suppose, although the farmer didn't recall seeing him before. Here it is."

Grant took the folded sheet she handed him, opened it and read:

Camera will feel mighty bad if he loses his holding.

The *if* was heavily underscored.

Jim Grant tore the sheet and tossed the fragments into the great fireplace.

146

"You're not going to marry Cale Whitmer," he stated flatly.

Lila glanced sideways at him through her lashes.

"Why?" She asked softly.

"Because I won't let you. Because I —" Grant began. He ceased speaking abruptly as Camera's step sounded in the hallway.

"Hello, Jim," the rancher greeted him as he entered the room. "Glad you dropped in. Saves me a trip down to your place to deliver an invitation."

"An invitation?"

"Yep," Camera said with a grin. "The fifteenth of the month comes next week, and it was on the fifteenth of this month that my grandfather founded Villa de Laredo, as he called it. After the community really got going, he always celebrated the anniversary date with a big *fiesta* as our Mexican friends call it; a costume ball with everybody present. My dad kept up the custom and so have I. Guess we might as well have the last one this year — the suit goes to trial on the twentieth, I believe," he added with a wry smile.

"Cam, stop it!" Lila said sharply. "We're going to celebrate many, many more anniversaries."

"Hope you're right," Camera returned. "Anyhow, we'll celebrate this one."

"We certainly will," Lila declared energetically. "What sort of a costume shall we get for Jim? A suit of armour such as was worn by the knights of old when they rescued damsels in distress would be appropriate, but I doubt if we can dig one up on short notice."

Camera studied Grant's build. "I've a notion General Santos Benavides' uniform would fit him," he said. "It's up in the attic somewhere, in one of the old trunks, I expect."

"That's it. He'll look fine as a Confederate General, although rather youthful."

"Promotion was fast in those days," Grant said, falling in with her humour.

"Okay, root it out," Camera said. "I'm riding to town with some of the boys. See you when I get back, Jim, sometime tonight."

"Come on, Jim, let's find that uniform!" Lila exclaimed. She led the way up flights of stairs, chattering gaily. Grant sensed that she preferred not to discuss Cale Whitmer's note at the moment, and he respected her wishes in the matter.

The attic was airy and well lighted by several windows, and crammed with the usual jumble to be found in attics. Lila surveyed several ancient-looking trunks lined against one wall.

"I'd say this is the oldest — it should be in here," she said, raising the lid. Kneeling beside the trunk, she began taking out articles of wearing apparel, masculine and feminine, all in the fashion of an earlier day.

"Here it is!" She exclaimed, drawing forth an old grey uniform with the stars of the Confederacy on the collar. She held up the long coat against Grant.

"Should fit you perfectly," she declared. "We have the sword, too. You'll look wonderful. Now let's see if I can find something to wear that will go with it."

148

She resumed her search and presently turned up a yellow brocade trimmed with seed pearls and cascades of lace.

"Don't know who this belonged to," she said, "but whoever she was, she wasn't very big. I believe I can wear it, with a few alterations. That is, unless I can find something I like better," she added, diving into the trunk again.

"Here are a lot of old papers," she said in a muffled voice, for her head was in the depths of the big trunk. She passed over her shoulder a thick bundle that crackled in her hand.

Grant took the papers, which appeared to be legal documents written in Spanish, which he could read fairly well. He glanced at the topmost idly, looked at a second.

Suddenly his hands tightened on the bundle. He leaned forward, peering, his eyes glowing. He began riffling through the packet, and all the while his excitement grew. Lila popped out of the trunk at his sharp exclamation.

"What's the matter?" She inquired apprehensively. "See a rat? I don't like rats."

Grant paid no attention but continued to scan the ancient documents. Lila stared at him in bewilderment. Finally he raised his eyes.

"Lila," he said, his voice a trifle unsteady, "come here and look at these things. Do you know what they are? They are mortgages and notes for money loaned by Don Tomas Sanchez to the people of Laredo and the surrounding country. There are dozens of them, all properly drawn and legal. And in nearly every one is mention of the land grant made to Tomas Sanchez by the Spanish King and approved by his agent and colonizer, Don Jose de Escandon, Count of Sierra Gorda."

"And what does it mean?" She asked, her blue eyes wide, her own voice trembling.

"It means," said Grant, "that right here is all the corroborative evidence Camera needs to secure his title. And it means more. These notes and mortgages are payable on demand and collectible, with the interest that has accumulated during the years, from the heirs of those who signed them. If he wants to, Camera can bankrupt half of Laredo!"

"Oh, Jim, he'd never do that!" Lila exclaimed. "But does it really mean his ranch is safe?"

"It sure does," Grant replied. "And it means, too, that you are safe from Cale Whitmer, although you never were in danger from him. I'd have taken care of that."

"Would you have, really?" She asked, the dimple showing at the corner of her mouth, but her eyes misty.

"Yes, darn it!" He answered. "Come here!"

He held out his arms. She swayed toward him, and at that moment boots pounded the floor downstairs and a voice shouted hoarsely:

"Jim! Jim Grant! Where are you, feller? Come a-running'! Pronto!"

CHAPTER
TWENTY-ONE

Lila went rigid, her eyes wide and staring. "That's Jess Sanborn," she said. "Oh, something terrible must have happened!"

"Let's go!" Grant said quietly. "Coming, Jess," he called to Sanborn. They hurried downstairs together and found Sanborn stamping about in the living room and breathing as if he had just run a race.

"The cook told me you were here," he shot at Grant. "Where the devil is everybody?"

"They're all up on the north pasture, except three or four who rode to town with Cam," Lila replied. "What's the matter, Jess?"

Sanborn swore. "Listen, Jim, one of Camera's nesters, a smart young feller, met him on the road and told him Cale Whitmer and a bunch have moved into the old ranch-house over to the west and aim to hold it. The nester said they got a writ of ejectment or something like that and aim to establish tenant's rights, whatever that means. I met the nester right after he met Camera — he was headed for town. He said Cam only had four of the boys with him but that he headed straight for the ranch house. I high-tailed it here to pick up the boys and get there ahead of him by a short cut I know. There's going to be trouble."

"Come on," Grant said. "I'll get my horse. Be seeing you, Lila." He rushed from the house and to the stable at a run. It took him only seconds to put the rig on Smoke and join Sanborn, who had mounted his own horse and was waiting.

Lila was on the veranda. "Take care of yourself, Jim," she called. The moment Grant and Sanborn were out of sight, she ran to the stable.

"If we can just get there ahead of him, I have something to tell him that should make him see reason," Grant said as they raced west.

"I hope so," said Sanford. "The nester said Cam looked like a crazy man. He's got a terrible temper, and he's really worked up. I'm afraid if we don't catch him there'll be a shooting, and Cam and the boys are outnumbered. But they've got to circle a patch of broken ground, and that may give us a chance. Sift sand, jughead; we've got places to go."

Sanford's big dun was a splendid animal, almost if not fully as good as Smoke. The miles flowed swiftly under the speeding hoofs. Sanford glanced at the lowering sky and shook his head.

"Overcast and getting dark early, and that ain't so good," he muttered. Grant said nothing and anxiously scanned the trail ahead.

The horses laboured up a long but gentle rise, reached the crest, sped across a level stretch to the opposite descent.

152

"There's the ranch house," said Sanford, gesturing toward a squat building set in a grove of live oaks.

"And look there," said Grant, pointing to a trail from the east. Along the trail a group of horsemen were speeding.

"It's them!" Exclaimed Sanford. "Feller, it's going to be close."

It was close; in fact, it was a dead heat. Grant and Sanford dashed up to the ranch house as Camera and his four cowboys were dismounting.

"Wait, Cam; I've got something to tell you," Grant shouted.

"Later," Camera flung over his shoulder. His face was set, his nostrils quivering. He bounded up the steps, crossed the veranda and flung open the door, his cowboys and Grant and Sanford crowding behind him.

In the room a couple of bracket lamps cast a warm glow. Seated at a table were Cale Whitmer, Whispering Shane and a big bearded man whom Grant instantly recognized as Lafe Haskins. Half a dozen of Whitmer's cowhands lounged about the room.

For a moment there was silence; then Camera Sanchez spoke.

"What the devil are you people doing here?" He demanded.

Cale Whitmer grinned provokingly. "We're occupying state land we intend to buy," he said.

"State land, nothing!" Camera exploded. "This is my property and you know it."

"Oh, no," Whitmer returned. "You're just a squatter and always have been. Yep, we're taking over — we got a court order."

Camera glared at him.

"You infernal thief —" he began.

Just how the ruckus started was never definitely established. Jess Sanford maintained one of Whitmer's cowhands drew a gun and pointed it at Camera. Anyhow, two shots rang out, and instantly the room rocked to a roar of gunfire.

In ten seconds it was all over. Grant, one sleeve shot to ribbons, the left side of his face crimson from a cheek wound, lowered his gun and peered in horror through the smoke.

The place was a shambles. Cale Whitmer was reeling and staggering across the room, clutching at his neck from which the blood was spurting in jets. He sagged against the door post and slid slowly down it. Camera Sanchez lay on his back, shot through the chest, blowing blood bubbles with every gasping breath. Six cowhands, three of Whitmer's and three from the Rafter S, were sprawled dead. Against the wall stood Whispering Shane and the remaining three Bradded R punchers, hands raised under the menace of Jess Sanborn's cocked gun.

Lafe Haskins, with six bullets in him, lay in the centre of the room, writhing in agony. In his mutilated right hand he still held a gun. Even as Grant started toward him, he raised the Colt and pointed it at Whispering Shane.

154

Grant bounded forward, but too late; Haskins pulled the trigger.

Garland Shane raised himself on his tiptoes, an awful look of incredulous disbelief on his face. His mouth opened, and for once he didn't whisper. His voice rose in a frightful shriek, he plunged forward on his face and lay still.

Lafe Haskins looked up at Grant. "I — learned to — trigger with — another — finger!" He panted, and died.

Grant motioned to the three Bradded R cowboys. "Let them go," he told Sanborn. "There's enough death here. See what you can do for your boss — I'm afraid it isn't much," he ordered them, and bent over Camera Sanchez.

Camera was unconscious but still breathing. Grant tore open his shirt and examined the wound, a small blue hole just below his right breast. Only a few drops of blood oozed from it, but the red froth on Camera's lips told of internal bleeding.

"There's a bed in the next room," said Sanborn. "Think we can risk carrying him to it?"

"Be best, I think," Grant said. "Then head for town and the doctor. Notify the sheriff and Judge Parkinson while you're at it. Tell the doctor to sift sand. If Cam is still alive when he gets here, I've a notion he may pull through. It's a lung wound and bad, but if it doesn't do for him right away, he's got a chance; he's young and tough as a pine knot."

Sanborn hurried from the house; the clatter of his horse's hoofs faded away into the distance.

155

Grant walked across to where Cale Whitmer lay, his three cowboys grouped helplessly about him. Whitmer's eyes were beginning to glaze, but he recognized Grant.

"Sorry, feller," he gurgled through the blood in his throat. "End of a crooked trail — never was crooked before. Bad, but never crooked — old paper in Shane's strongbox — Haskins stole it — you get it. Tell Lila — sorry that —"

His voice trailed away and he lasped into unconsciousness. Three minutes later he was dead.

Grant folded the dead hands across Whitmer's breast and straightened up. His voice was tired and dull when he spoke to the Bradded R hands.

"You fellows might as well head back to your ranch-house and get a wagon to pack him and the others home," he said. "I suppose the sheriff will want to talk to you, and also the rest of us, but I doubt if anything much will come of it."

As the cowboys turned to go, hoofs clattered to a sliding halt outside. A moment later Lila burst into the room, her eyes wild and fearful. She ran to Grant and clutched him with both hands.

"Oh, darling, are you all right?" She asked, her voice unsteady. "Oh, you're bleeding! Your face is cut!"

"Just a scratch," Grant told her, holding her close and patting her shoulder, "but I'm afraid Cam is in a bad way. Come on and look at him."

They entered the room where Camera had been placed on the bed. He was unconscious, his face livid, his breath coming in stertorous gasps, but the blood no longer frothed on his lips and his heartbeat, while weak, was steady.

"I believe he'll pull out of it," Grant predicted. "All we can do is wait for the doctor. Yes, Whitmer is dead, and Whispering Shane and several others."

A sudden thought struck him. He led the girl to where Lafe Haskins lay.

"Give him the once-over and try to recall if you have ever seen him before," he said.

Lila shuddered but obeyed, leaning close to the dead face. "He looks familiar," she said. "It seems to me I've seen him before, but I can't be sure."

"Suppose he wasn't wearing a beard," Grant prompted. Again she studied Haskins' set features.

"I believe it comes to me now," she said. "I think he is a man who once worked for Camera, about a year ago, I'd say. Yes, I'm sure he once rode for the Rafter S."

Grant nodded with satisfaction. "Thought so," he said. "And I'm willing to bet a hatful of pesos that he stole the grant from the drawer in which it was kept. Whitmer said before he died that it is in Shane's strongbox. Well, it doesn't matter any more. There's nobody left to press the suit, even against the corroborative evidence we now have. I hope the doctor gets here in a hurry!"

The wait for the doctor's arrival seemed long to the anxious watchers by Camera's bedside. Belated Rafter S punchers squatted on the floor nearby, talking together in low tones, for nobody cared to sit in the grisly outer room. Grant had thought it best not to remove the bodies until the sheriff got a look at them.

Finally, after an eternity of waiting, wheels sounded on the gravel outside the house. Another moment and the doctor entered, accompanied by Sheriff Foster, Judge Parkinson, and a woman. Grant stared. It was Norma Whitmer. Without glancing to either side, she walked to the bed and gazed down into Camera Sanchez' ashen face. Lila slipped an arm about her waist.

"He'll make it, Norma," she comforted the girl, adding hesitantly, "Cale is dead."

"Is he?" Norma answered without raising her eyes from Camera.

The doctor hurried forward, opening his bag of medicines and instruments. His examination was swift.

"Mighty bad hurt," was his verdict, "but he's young and hardy. I think we can pull him through, with care and good nursing."

"He'll get both," Norma said quietly. "You won't move him, Doctor?"

The practitioner shook his head. "Chances are it would kill him if we did," he replied. "We'll leave him right where he is. Lend me a hand, now, and we'll undress him and put him to bed so I can do some work on him."

"There," he said some time later. "I've done all I can. Now it's up to him — and you women." He led Grant to the outer room, where the sheriff was waiting.

"Well, Doc, you're coroner. I suppose you'll hold an inquest," Foster remarked.

158

"Oh, I suppose so, but I don't see any sense in it," Doc Beard replied with a grunt. "Seems nobody knows who shot who, and two or three of those who cashed in their chips we can very well do without. Chances are the jury'll hold it was suicide or accidental death or something like that."

Which, in effect, was the jury's verdict the following afternoon.

"Judge," Grant said to Parkinson, "it's late, but if you don't mind I'd like you to ride to the hacienda with me; you can spend the night there. I have something to show you. Jess," he told Sanborn, "you and the boys stay here to lend a hand if needed. What about you, Lila?"

"I'm staying with Norma," she replied quietly.

Grant nodded. She clung to him for a moment as he kissed her goodbye.

"I hate to let you out of my sight," she murmured. "I had such a hard, hard time tying onto you."

"Rats!" He scoffed. "You knew you had me hogtied the first time you saw me. I should have known it, too, but I guess a man's sort of dumb about such things. Good night, honey; see you tomorrow."

At the Rafter S ranch house, Judge Parkinson read the old documents with the greatest care, having Grant translate some of the passages to make sure they were in agreement. Finally he laid the papers aside, took off his spectacles and wiped them.

"Jim," he said, "if Camera Sanchez is of a mind to even up a few scores, this will make mighty sad reading for quite a lot of people."

"It's up to Camera," Grant replied, and did not comment further.

For three days Camera Sanchez hovered between life and death. However, once he passed the crisis his recovery was rapid.

"But if it hadn't been for that red-headed gal he would have taken the big jump," the doctor declared. "I don't believe she had a wink of sleep for seventy-two hours. She never left him for a minute. And I reckon she never will," he added with a chuckle.

A little over two weeks after that dreadful night in the old ranch house, there was a meeting of Laredo businessmen and other citizens that packed the great living room of the Rafter S hacienda. Present, also, were Jim Grant, Judge Parkinson and old Joel Collison, beside whom sat an elderly gentleman with a kindly face who was dressed in sober black. Over to one side sat Norma Whitmer, Lila McCarthy and several of the older Rafter S hands, including Jess Sanborn. In a chair by a table on which was a stack of old documents sat Camera Sanchez, looking rather pale but otherwise fit enough.

For a long moment Camera was silent, studying the faces before him. Then he spoke.

"Gentlemen," he said, "you all know why I have asked you to come here today — Judge Parkinson has told you. I have just a few words to say. I am convinced that my grandfather, Tomas Sanchez, never intended to call in the money these notes represent. Times were hard in those days, and the money he generously

160

loaned was to help folks who needed help. I am sure he got the greatest of pleasure from helping those in need. Whether or not my father, Jose Sanchez, knew of the existence of these mortgages, I cannot say, but I am confident he did. He did not call for the money due him, and it would be strange if I did not follow in the footsteps of my forebears."

He turned in his chair. "Lila," he called.

The blue-eyed girl came forward, smiling a little. "You know what to do," Camera said.

Lila picked up the bundle of papers and deposited them in the big fireplace. She took the lighted match Jim Grant handed her and touched the flame to the ancient documents. The flame sputtered for a moment, caught, died down, flared up and burned brightly. Soon there remained only a little heap of ashes and a few sparks that winked out one by one. A collective sigh went up; then Camera was fairly mobbed by men who pushed forward to shake his hand.

Gradually the gathering broke up, until there remained only the two girls, Jim Grant, Joel Collison, the Rafter S hands and the elderly gentleman in black to keep Camera company.

"Now I have something else to say," Camera stated, smiling broadly. "If it hadn't been for Jim Grant, things might have been quite different today. He and Lila will need a place to live, so I'm deeding the old ranch house and ten thousand acres to them as a wedding present."

"That's mighty fine of you, Camera," old Joel broke in, "but it really ain't necessary. That would place Jim too darned far away from me. I'm building him a house next to mine down on the Swinging J. He'll need to be around to keep an eye on things, for after all, it won't be long — I'm an old man — till he'll have the whole chore of running the spread on his hands."

He waved away all thanks and turned to the elderly gentleman in black.

"I sort of figured he'd be needed, so I brought Reverend Hammond along with me," he said. "Cam, you'd better stay sitting down, but Norma can stand beside you with Jim and Lila. Okay, Reverend, it's all yours."

The clergyman stood up and produced a book which he opened at a certain page. "Dearly beloved —" he began.

ABOUT THE AUTHOR

Leslie Scott was born in Lewisburg, West Virginia. During the Great War, he joined the French Foreign Legion and spent four years in the trenches. In the 1920s he worked as a mining engineer and bridge builder in the western American states and in China before settling in New York. A bar-room discussion in 1934 with Leo Margulies, who was managing editor for Standard Magazines, prompted Scott to try writing fiction. He went on to create two of the most notable series characters in Western pulp magazines. In 1936, Standard Magazines launched, and in *Texas Rangers*, Scott under the house name of **Jackson Cole** created Jim Hatfield, Texas Ranger, a character whose popularity was so great with readers that this magazine featuring his adventures lasted until 1958. When others eventually began contributing Jim Hatfield stories, Scott created another Texas Ranger hero, Walt Slade, better known as *El Halcon*, the Hawk, whose exploits were regularly featured in *Thrilling Western*. In the 1950s Scott moved quickly into writing book-length adventures about both Jim Hatfield and Walt Slade in long series of original paperback Westerns. At the same time, however, Scott was also doing some of his best work in hardcover Westerns published by Arcadia House; thoughtful, well-constructed stories, with engaging characters and authentic settings and situations. Among the best of these, surely, are *Silver City* (1953), *Longhorn Empire* (1954), *The Trail Builders* (1956), and *Blood on the Rio Grande* (1959). In these hardcover Westerns, many of which have never been reprinted, Scott proved himself highly capable of writing traditional Western stories with characters who have sufficient depth to change in the course of the narrative and with a degree of authenticity and historical accuracy absent from many of his series stories.